Montana Grace

Praise for Montana Grace

To write a great book, an author has to get so many things right: plot, pacing, compelling sentences, characters you care about, and ideally, a message that matters. Elizabeth Bradshaw has mastered all of these and produced a book that is great. It's moving, and a person reading it feels he or she is in the hands of a professional.

Mitzi Perdue, (Mrs. Frank Perdue) author, speaker, businesswoman

In *Montana Grace*, Elizabeth Bradshaw weaves an intricate tale of child sex trafficking, relationships, and redemption. Momentum builds as the story progresses, with plot twists enhancing the engrossing saga. Though dealing with a dark and difficult topic, Ms. Bradshaw avoids seamy details and brings us a drama infused with hope and a beautiful illustration of God bringing beauty from ashes. *Montana Grace* reminds us that no segment of society is safe from the tragic results of human trafficking. It involves those around us. Those we least expect.

Derri Smith, founder and CEO Emeritus of AncoraTN

With America waking up to the harsh tragedy of human trafficking being revealed in the last few years, Elizabeth Bradshaw has weaved a timely story of moving from disaster to God's grace. No matter what you've done or what's been done to you, everything can be changed for healing and reformation. *Montana Grace* is a story of hope and healing.

Gigi Butler, creator, and founder of Gigi's Cupcakes

I've been in a book club for over a year and read many books. For a season we had a few really good books then hit a dry spell. I have multiple books I can't seem to finish. Saying all that to say, I was not able to put this book down. I carried the story through my day pondering and looking forward to the next opportunity to read. I felt so many emotions throughout the story. It evoked fear, anger and even some personal pain. I thought I had a deep understanding of forgiveness until I read *Montana Grace*.

Shannon Bell, Nashville, TN

Montana Grace is a compelling story of the resilience of the human spirit -- and much more. It is not a comfortable story, but it's one that grabbed my heart and inspired me with the courageous persistence and positivity of the key characters. I want to be challenged to be a more informed and better person when I read, and *MG* certainly did that for me with its admirable characters, like those who helped Tana "get back on her feet." Parts of *Montana Grace* are very difficult to read, and I appreciate that Elizabeth Bradshaw wasn't too graphic. But the details she did give were so realistic.

Millie Samuelson, Rapid City, SD

Montana Grace

Elizabeth Bradshaw

NEW YORK

LONDON • NASHVILLE • MELBOURNE • VANCOUVER

Montana Grace

Published in New York, New York, by Morgan James Publishing. Morgan James is a trademark of Morgan James, LLC. www.MorganJamesPublishing.com

Proudly distributed by Ingram Publisher Services.

Scripture taken from THE HOLY BIBLE, NEW INTERNATIONAL VERSION ®. Copyright© 1973, 1978, 1984, 2011 by Biblica, Inc.™. Used by permission of Zondervan.

Publisher's Note: This novel is a work of fiction. Names, characters, places, and incidents are either products of the author's imagination or used fictitiously. All characters are fictional, and any similarity to people living or dead is purely coincidental.

Morgan James BOGO™

A **FREE** ebook edition is available for you or a friend with the purchase of this print book.

CLEARLY SIGN YOUR NAME ABOVE

Instructions to claim your free ebook edition:
1. Visit MorganJamesBOGO.com
2. Sign your name CLEARLY in the space above
3. Complete the form and submit a photo of this entire page
4. You or your friend can download the ebook to your preferred device

ISBN 9781631959271 paperback
ISBN 9781631959288 ebook
Library of Congress Control Number:
2022935953

Cover Design & Interior Design by:
Christopher Kirk
www.GFSstudio.com

Cover Photo by:
PETER MÜLLER
© [2017]

Informational Graphics by:
Tony Bradshaw

Morgan James PUBLISHING Builds with... **Habitat for Humanity®** Peninsula and Greater Williamsburg

Morgan James is a proud partner of Habitat for Humanity Peninsula and Greater Williamsburg. Partners in building since 2006.

Get involved today! Visit MorganJamesPublishing.com/giving-back

For the Maker of wide open skies and glorious sunsets.

Acknowledgments

Tony, always an adventure. Thank you for seeing the best in me when I couldn't see it myself. I love you, always!

Jonathan, Gabriele, Stefanie, Kaileigh, Abigayle, and Nicholas—I know this book was as much work for you as it was for me. Thanks for being willing to let me work. I love you!

Alan and Barb, Wade and Judy, Dan and Leila, Angelia, and Grandma Bethie—For all you have taught me, encouraged me, supported me, and believed in me, I am forever grateful. I love you!

Kara, thank you for some of the best conversations, for helping me understand the importance of sunsets, and discovering what the key really means. You are the true treasure. (If you would like to get in on Kara's wisdom, check out her chapter "Honoring Your Value" in the book *Pebbles in the Pond, Wave 4*.)

Alice, Camille, Gayle, Jenny, Julia, Karen, Kimberly, Laura, Lisa, Lonnie, Macy, Melinda M., Melinda V., Mila, Naomi, Paula, Penny—I couldn't have asked for better support when I needed it most. Thank you for being my cheering section.

Millie, I am grateful to have sat under your teaching when I was just learning who God is. Thank you for being a wonderful example of kindness and humility.

Kristen and Jessi, your leadership has been a Godsend. Thank you for following His lead, being in my corner, helping me out of the mire, and finding my voice.

Lee and Sonja, I am grateful God used the two of you to push me over the writer's edge! Without you, there wouldn't be a *Montana Grace*!

Anna Floit, editor at The Peacock Quill, I would be a mess without you! Thank you for all your hard work and patience with me!

Morgan James, David, Heidi, Gayle, Cortney, and the amazing team surrounding me—thank you for your belief, support, and encouragement.

Prologue

Washington, DC, 1991

With a flash of light and a swirl of smoke, the extra-long matches burst to life, illuminating the cigar-stuffed sneer on his lips with an eerie glow in the otherwise inky night. Dark shadows danced with hot highlights as the tiny flames flickered and jumped around the sideways stick.

Before him, the small car butted nose-first against the tree along the currently deserted park road. A lone female body lay in a crumpled heap a few yards away.

Surveying the scene with great satisfaction, the broad-shouldered man leaned on the front of the police car. He slowly rotated the cigar 360 degrees allowing the yellow flames to lightly caress the cigar butt as it began to burn.

Devin Shire pulled wipes from a small bag in the cruiser's trunk and quickly cleaned off the blood, careful to not let it dry. He removed his blood-stained white tank and replaced it with a new one from the bag before sliding his light blue uniform shirt in place. He picked up the bloody tank top and used wipes before he closed the trunk lid.

Behind the cruiser, a small SUV, with its engine running, used its headlights to light the scene.

"D-D-D-Devin?" the thin driver with wireframe glasses called from the window.

"Yeah, Henry?"

"Um . . . if you don't need anything else, I'm going to go back to the office and wait for you to call for the coroner." Devin acknowledged with a tip of his head. "I, uh, I'll take the cargo to the safe house."

"I'll let him know." The driver nodded and pulled the gearshift into reverse, allowing the car and its timid driver to make their escape.

"Shire," the man with the match turned his attention to the officer as the SUV pulled away. "Are you ready?" Devin affirmed, carrying a small black box and wires to the front of the car. "Good. Where is the body?"

"In the back seat, sir," Shire confirmed as he watched the larger man rub his chest. "Are you okay, Boss?"

"What?" he asked absentmindedly, before noticing his fingers were massaging the area the seatbelt had crossed his chest. "Oh. Yes, I'll probably have a few bruised ribs from that little move, but I'm fine." Devin simply shook his head in understanding, as the man continued, chuckling. "I hit the tree a little harder than I intended. I guess I wanted to be sure the car was well damaged."

"That you did, sir."

"Did we miss anything?"

"No, sir. He is in the back of the car, she is on the ground, and your used cigar is on the passenger floorboard."

He took a long drag from the burning cigar before answering, "Perfect. Then let's get on with it. That new senator from New Hampshire is giving my firm a run for our money." He shook his head, "that man is always getting into trouble we have to clean up." He sneered at the thought as it crossed his mind. "I may even have to replace him with West."

"Yes, sir." Devin agreed, though the idea of West as a senator made him laugh. He moved closer and nestled the box into the gravel near the car's undercarriage. Tossed quickly through the backseat window, the tank top and used wipes scattered without complaint across the lifeless body nestled in the backseat. The smell of gas hung heavy in the air, and Devin didn't want to stay long. Smelling like gas when other officers, or the fire department, arrived wouldn't be acceptable. Quickly, he made his way back to his boss, now standing a few hundred feet away.

Gesturing toward the remote control in Devin's hand, the man demanded, "You are confident this will work?"

"Completely. There are enough fumes to light, and since they are outside the car, the fireball will be quick, and the flames will burn hot. This launch control has a range of about five hundred feet. I took the kids to shoot rockets yesterday, and it sparked perfectly. There shouldn't be any trouble."

The sneer returned to his boss's lips. "Show me."

With slight pressure from his thumb, the wires near the car sparked, exploding the fumes to life, flames quickly engulfing the small car as thick black smoke billowed into the air.

"Excellent, Shire," the sneering man admitted. He turned to face the officer. "Did you see where the box went?"

Devin shrugged as he answered, "If I don't find it now, I'll pick it up when I gather evidence."

"No screw-ups, Shire."

"There won't be any."

The radio at Devin's hip crackled to life, "Adam 4321?"

"4321. Go ahead, dispatch."

"We have a 10-73 in the Piney Branch Park area. Approximate location of Park Road North West."

"10-4. Please dispatch Engine 11, Truck 6 also. It sounds like we might have a fire in the park. I'm on my way."

Central Illinois, 2001

The light glazed her eyes in shock. They always did. And yet somehow, even through the thick mental haze, she could tell this time was different. Somewhere behind the large looming shadowy figure in the doorway were loud, chaotic voices—men's voices. It was always men entering her dimly lit room.

The man in the doorway wore much better clothing than the usual fare who crossed her threshold. When he spoke, his inflection was softer, his tone comforting, and his approach slower and more gentle than any man since . . . since she could remember. She grappled with the confusion coursing through her mind and cowered from his reach. Still, his approach was soft, soothing, almost inviting. So unfamiliar.

Without warning, in a fluid motion of legs and arms, he gathered her small frame like a rag doll to his chest. And yet, this hold, this touch, was not the same as any of the other men. Her skin quivered under the cool touch as his jacket swaddled her. This feeling clashed against the usually abrasive feel of calloused working man's hands. In lieu of old sweat, stale coffee, and rotting teeth, her nose flooded with the scents of soap, aftershave, and fresh air as he carried her outside, as much a shock as the bright sunlight.

Once outside, Doorway Man headed toward the waiting ambulance. A woman in a dark uniform paced in front of the open doors, anticipating their arrival.

"Hey, sweet girl. I'm Agent Paul Masters, and this is Ms. Michelle. We like to call her Mitch, with an M," a sly smile slid across his lips. "She is an EMT, which means she's trained to help hurting people, and she will take good care of you." He lay her down on the gurney inside the ambulance, where Mitch, with an M, began to look the little girl over. Agent Masters walked toward his car.

After her initial assessment, Michelle found him heading back her way, two coffee cups in his hands. They stopped in front of the ambulance, where he handed one cup to her. Her whispers were less to keep her voice from being heard and more to keep it under control.

"Looks like this one is eight, maybe nine." Truth be told, she was twelve, but it would be a while before anyone knew that. "She has endured drugs; her arm shows scarring from forced needle marks. The scar on her face is a couple of years old, based on its healing rate. Her body presents several signs of undernourishment. I bet she doesn't weigh fifty pounds, Paul."

"I figured," Agent Paul Masters, could hardly contain his disgust as he started back toward the young girl. "The bag of dog food I feed Samson weighs more than she does, Mitch," he hissed at her.

"I know, Paul. But she's alive. We'll make sure she gets back on her feet."

Agent Masters rounded the back of the ambulance, where the little girl still rested on a stretcher. Before he spoke, he reestablished his presence with his soothing voice, slipping back into the softer tone, much like shifting into a higher gear to ease the stress on an engine.

"Sweet girl, Ms. Mitch will be riding with you to the hospital now." As Agent Masters spoke, his free hand took Michelle's, and he eased her up into the ambulance. "There, a team of doctors and nurses are going gently examine you to make sure you recover strongly. Ms.

Chapter 1

Tana Jensen sat across the table from Derby Cooper. Being close to people always made her feel uncomfortable, yet she knew it was just part of the job. Being that close to Derby was enough to make her skin crawl. Part of the job or not, she did not enjoy where she found herself.

Derby, a partner in the Cooper, Street, and Irons Law Firm, began his deposition. "For the record, Ms. Jensen, please state the details of your job."

"As part of the FBI's Cyber Division, I am in the local cyber squad. It's my job to root out the bad guys and find the children. To pull them out of horrible situations."

"By bad guys you mean . . ."

"People who sell kids for sex."

"People do that?"

Something about the question made Tana snicker, though she couldn't decide if it was nerves or irritation. "Come on, Mr. Cooper; you know they do. The reality is there are probably two million children currently being held against their will as sex slaves worldwide. That doesn't include people who use kids because of the power they hold over them in, say, an acting or political job. So yes, people do that."

Derby chose to ignore the dig and pushed on with his questions. "So how do you fit in this?"

"I use the computer to filter and fine-tune the selection of children for sex to rescue them from that life of misery."

"How, precisely?"

"The use of the internet. In today's world, it's so much easier for children to be bought and sold, simply with some of the same websites people use to sell their unwanted things. I act as an arm of law enforcement to try and navigate the massive online commercial sex market to find children and identify their traffickers. Technology is our tool to address this aspect of the crime. Every day, there are over a hundred thousand new escort ads posted online. Woven throughout that data are children, being bought and sold online for sexual use."

"And how, exactly, do you see Senator Henry West fitting into this?"

Tana watched him, the details of the case whirling through her head. The imagery of photos of the senator and his son and a small, scared little boy continued to shake her core.

"Ms. Jensen?" Derby tried to get her attention, uncomfortable with her silence.

Tana sighed. "When one has been through as much as I have, you learn what to look for as a means of self-preservation. Men like him become experts at targeting and exploiting children," she answered the question.

"A gut reaction?" He could hardly control his sneer.

Unwilling to give all details so soon, Tana shrugged, "If that's what you want to call it."

"What else would you call it?"

"Expertise."

"Expertise?" The word smacked with bitterness in Derby's mouth. "And just what exactly are you an expert in?"

Tana sat back in the chair. She knew this man. Or his type. It was getting harder and harder to tell the difference. "I know how scummy men react to feeling cornered, and I am on a mission to remove scummy men from their freedom."

Derby matched her casual body language with his own. His words, however, were not casual. "Just what are you trying to say, Ms. Jensen?"

"I'm saying I want to see such men in prison. How much clearer can I get?"

Without permission from his lawyer, Senator West spoke for the first time since Tana entered the room, his voice an even tempo and chillingly calm. "If you keep prosecuting me this way, Ms. Jensen . . . if you keep doing this," he waved his hand in the air as if brushing away an invisible fly, "someone is going to get hurt."

Los Angeles, 2016

"Greg!" His mother called down the stairs, frustrated he wasn't already at the door. She took the afternoon off work for this, so at least he could be ready on time. "Come on, son. We need to be in the car if we are going to make it to the audition on time."

"I'm coming," he called back, as he checked his look in the mirror once more. The role called for a baseball-loving boy. Personally, Greg preferred football, but his mom had picked up a Dodgers cap and T-shirt for this call. The bright blue cap made his eyes look darker than they normally were. He adjusted the hat over his blond curls, flipping them around the cap's edge.

"Gregory Owen Blakely!"

Startled by the use of his full name, Greg decided that was as good as it was going to get and hurried from his bedroom. Taking the stairs two at a time to the top, he picked up his script and started out the front door.

A single mother for the last year, Silvia Blakely had been told by more than one stranger in the grocery store she should have Greg in modeling or movies. Watching the smiling boy bound up the stairs, she was pretty sure it was his dimples and the sparkle in those clear blue eyes.

"Stan is going to be irritated if we are late since he had to work so hard to get you this audition." Stan West, a well-known child actor agent, was the reason she decided it might be time to try getting Greg into acting. What could it hurt? If he were able to get a small job or two, it sure would help with the bills. Dare she even think, maybe even help pay for college? As her boy grabbed the script off the small entryway table, a folder caught her eyes. "Shoot. I thought I gave those to Renee." She picked the folder up and moved to lock the door as she continued, "I'm going to have to drop you off and run back by the office."

"Sounds good, Mom."

Silvia pulled the keys from the door and fished her phone from her purse, searching for a number as she walked.

"Chuck Blue. What can I do for you?"

His corny greeting made her giggle to herself. "Hey, it's more like what I can do for you. I found the file for the Bale shoot on my table. I'll bring it by as soon as I drop Greg off."

Georgia, 2001

Driving into the parking lot and walking to the building was always gloomy. Even on a summer day as warm and sunny as this, a cloud still shrouded Millie Jensen's soul like an icy wet blanket. Oh, how she longed to break through that blackness. Shatter it like a stuck window, and let in the fresh air. Her heart ached to feel alive again. Hungered for the life absent these last eight years. Much like a healed surgery scar is still numb, life moves on, rebuilds, grows stronger, and is not so tender. Nonetheless, there is always a senseless, yet nagging, area. A reminder that to continue is not to be as you once were. Maybe that ache was a good thing, she thought. A small sign she was still alive and not as cold and spiritless as she sometimes felt.

To the casual onlooker, Millie Jensen appeared calm as she made her way into the Georgia State Prison. Any observer would feel she had it all together in her slacks and silk blouse, her once-auburn-but-now-graying hair moving softly in the Georgia breeze. Her once deep jade eyes had mellowed into an icy green shade over the last several years, though most who knew her now didn't know the difference.

In reality, thoughts whipped and swirled like a bowl full of uncooked scrambled eggs through Millie's mind. Her faithful companion, nervousness, still would not let her make this journey alone, even though she'd been coming for four years now. Currently, it clung to her like a wet T-shirt. She was unable to put her finger on the reason. Today was just like any other third Saturday of any other month. Catching a glimpse of a desk calendar as she handed the guard her ID, her heart sank. Oh, yeah. She knew it was close but had failed to foresee the anniversary would be today. If she had anticipated it better, she would have skipped this trip.

Eight years today.

After the first couple of years, Millie found it so much easier to not watch the calendar every day. Or even at all for around two weeks before the anniversary. If she didn't know the exact date and kept herself busy, she could maintain a level of normalcy. This façade allowed the people around her to be comfortable. She was so tired of the looks of pity and lack of grace from the people who were supposed to be friends. Tired of judgment for the pain she had no control over and no way to rid herself of.

Observing the standard routine, her body moved through the mechanics of check-in. Identification and keys handed over to the guard and on through the metal detector. She learned long ago not to bring a purse or bag with her. As she moved, Millie's thoughts were years away, swept up in the warmth of that beautiful summer day. She could almost touch Montana's sweet face, feel her warm breath on her cheek. See her dancing with her shadow and laughing with her daddy.

Eight years. How has it already been eight years? Montana would be twelve now. Almost a teenager. A tween, isn't that what they called it these days? Sassy. Sweet. Stubborn like her daddy. The mental image brought a smile to Millie's face. Those captivating green eyes, so much like her own had been long ago . . . Was her hair still sun bleached? Maybe it was darker now.

Twelve.

"Mrs. Jensen." The voice of the guard handing back her ID and car keys, along with her visitor's pass snapped her back to reality.

Millie found a smile for him. "Thank you, Officer Jackson. How are the wife and kids?"

Officer D.R. Jackson returned the grin. "Kids are growing like weeds. And my wife is much better now; thank you." Millie acknowledged the information with a nod. Four years of the same routine allows one to know the people you come in contact with each trip.

Washington, DC, 2018

The familiar melody of her ringtone both startled and comforted her. She looked away from the computer monitor and focused on the face of her phone. A small smile slid across her lips. That realization made her pause. . . . Who was the last person she let close enough to make her smile? How long ago was that? She pressed a button and brought the phone to her ear, "Hello."

"Hello, beautiful." She could feel her body ease from the softness of his voice.

"Hi, charming."

"How are you feeling today?"

She nonchalantly stroked the faded scar on her cheek. "Well enough to spend the day at Cooper's office."

"Ouch."

"Oh, well. At least I am not repulsed by the thought of food now. Having the flu helps me keep my girlish figure."

Tate let out a soft chuckle. "Have plans for tonight?"

"Maybe."

"Hmmm. I wonder what your answer would be if I suggested picking you up for dinner in three hours."

Tana found herself touching her face again and picked up a pen to keep her fingers busy. "I don't know that I'm ready to go out."

"Hmmm," he said again. "Are you up for a night in then? We also need to go over some of the details concerning Greg Blakely. And I want to hear how it went at Derby's office."

She groaned, "Suddenly, it's all work with you?"

"Of course not. I hate when you are sick and I don't get to be with you. It makes me lose all focus on what matters. Work is just an excuse you can't brush off easily. I just want to see those eyes of yours."

She laughed. "That sounds more like you. I might be able to pull that off."

"Great. Don't do anything. I'll bring dinner. What time would you like me to arrive?"

"I've probably got two more hours of work for Derby. And I would like to shower before you get here. Three hours sounds good."

"Ah," he teased, "so I should be there in two hours."

"Only if you want to find the door locked."

"Yes, ma'am. See you soon."

Washington, DC, 1991

The low crackling of the radio was merely background noise for the scene in front of him. John hadn't genuinely listened to any of it as he watched the sun rise behind the home holding his attention. The smooth vocals began to crack his concentration. Aretha Franklin and George Michael together were unmistakable, and the lyrics took his mind back several years.

Warriors fighting.

Battles won.

Victory.

He could see them all there together as if it had been the night before, instead of what, almost five years ago now? The battles of law school successfully won. Of the four young men sitting around the bar table that night, John Palmer knew she would end up with him. Not that he was an arrogant guy. Far from it. John was the average, run-of-the-mill, blue-eyed, dark-haired, athletic type. More of a base-ball build—for sure not a football build. Smart, funny, and self-deprecating to some extent.

Carleigh was beyond beautiful. Presumably, she had some Scandinavian lineage somewhere. Her elegance was effortless, her presence intoxicating. Everyone on campus knew Carleigh could be a model if she were so inclined—except Carleigh, who thought she was no beauty at all. Striking looks, the pronounced jawline outlining her face, framed by flowing red curls and punctuated by light brown eyes.

Though in some light, or maybe it was determined by her mood, they held an almost green tint. John found her intelligence and wit to be as attractive as her appearance. She was simply stunning. Watching Carleigh talk with the other guys, he knew she had her eye on him, though he wasn't sure why.

Remembering their history from the cover of a dark sedan, John watched the house Carleigh entered that crisp fall morning. Still watching an hour later, he waited for her to walk back out. Even now, four years into the marriage, he couldn't figure out why she had picked him in college. He and his brother, Lee, were just your regular guys in law school. The other two chaps in their group were Belmont Cooper and his younger brother, Derby. Those boys came from money, (though as a child, John just understood his aunt and uncle had lots of horses). John always felt that made the Cooper boys more appealing. Carleigh, being at once kind to them and still blowing them off in favor of him, was a mystery he intended to solve.

Now, sitting in the cramped confines of the surveillance car, he wasn't sure he would ever know.

He let the music drag his mind back to that celebration in the bar, the night they found out they had all passed their law bar. He could almost hear the ring of Belmont's knife on the champagne glass. "Here's to the finest group of new lawyers this side of textbooks! I am looking forward to working with—and against—you ladies and gentlemen!" Belmont toasted the group.

"Hear, hear!" Sitting around the crowded table was the group of kids with whom he had spent the last three years: four guys—John, Belmont, Derby, Lee—spending time with four ladies—Carleigh, Sonja, Amelia, and Georgia. They had become fast friends at the start of law school. Of course, it helped that the boys were cousins, John and Lee twins (though not identical), Belmont and Derby were two years apart in age but entered law school together. The last six months had changed things. Friends created deeper relationships or drifted off to their own worlds, joining different groups on campus and spending time apart.

As Aretha Franklin and George Michael belted their duet through the speakers that night—the tune she called *their song*—Carleigh jumped up and demanded, "Come on, John! Dance with me!" He was happy to acquiesce.

Happy to be her warrior fighting.

Happy to win battles for her.

Winning her heart, his biggest victory.

She danced and sang along, her uncontainable joy spilling over onto him. He had to smile, and even laugh, as she sang along and moved to the rhythm. With every move, Carleigh mesmerized him. The rest of the world faded, and she was all he could see. Before the song ended, John grabbed her and pulled her body tight against his own. Without a word, his lips found hers in the middle of the dance floor.

Leaning back to look into his eyes, her arms finding their way around his neck, she asked, "What was that for?"

"Because I love you."

"Ohhh, well, thank you very much." She smiled at him.

"No, I'm serious. I am totally in love with you, Carleigh. And I want to spend the rest of my life with you."

She cocked her head to the side, "John Palmer, did you just ask me to marry you?"

"Not officially," he grinned. "Just letting you in on my plans." He kissed her again. "I want to make sure you don't go anywhere with anyone else."

"The only place I'm going is back to the table for a drink. Come on." She took his hand, and they pushed through the crowded dance floor to the table to find Lee and Belmont bickering with each other.

"Oh, I look forward to those battles, Belmont," Lee grinned. "I'm going to kick your—"

"Lee!" John laughed out of frustration; he was never sure what that boy was thinking. "Save your arguing for the courtroom. You two will be at each other soon enough."

"Lighten up, John! Belmont knows I'm just picking on him. I'll save my strongest argument for when I need to put his clients in jail."

"I can see where this is going." Carleigh stepped into the conversation and leaned between the brothers. "You two are going to end up throwing punches soon. Come on, John; take me home so I can get some rest, please."

The slamming of the screen door closing startled John from his memory. He watched Carleigh turn back to the house and speak to someone through the mesh, her smile brighter than it had been at home recently, then turn toward her car. He watched her climb in, tinker for a few moments (probably choosing a CD to suit her mood, if he knew his wife), and press the brake as she started the engine. After she moved, John put his vehicle into drive, made a U-turn, and headed in the same direction.

Washington, DC, 2018

With the knock on her door came the flutter of butterflies in Tana's stomach. She smoothed her shirt, tossed her dark hair out of her face, and crossed the carpet. Deep breath, hand on the door. She turned the knob. "Good evening."

"Hello, beautiful. Hungry?"

"Actually, charming, I am. Come in." Tate walked into the room and went straight to the table, where he placed the cartons of Thai food, as Tana shut the door. He turned, took two strides to her side, and scooped her into his arms, kissed her cheek, and held her tight. She could feel his chest rise and fall, his breath on her neck, his hand in her hair. She held onto his neck and allowed herself to breathe in his fresh scent. With the fall of her chest, Tana could feel her body releasing the day's pressure and strain into his arms.

"I have been longing to hold you close all day. Missed you."

"I would have missed you too, except you kept calling," Tana teased him.

"Oh? I've got to watch that, or I'll give away my secret." As he spoke, Tana noticed the features she loved so much. The way his mop of dark hair framed his face, the five o'clock shadow he didn't bother to erase. Those piercing, ice-blue eyes. Spellbound by his monologue, she did not interrupt him. "That I think I am in love with you, Montana Grace." He put a finger to his lips, "Shhh."

"Shhh?" Tana playfully pushed back from his chest. "Any man who thinks he's in love with me better be ready to tell people."

"Ah, then I'll get my rock-climbing gear." He let go of his grip on her and flung wide his arms. "'Cuz I want to shout it from the mountaintops!" Tana giggled at his dramatics. "You just say the word, and I'll make it official."

"I don't know about you, but I'm hungry." Even as she walked away, she could feel the pain in his eyes. Confusion flooded her soul, and she fought an urge to run when his hand brushed hers. When would she stop wanting to run?

"Tana?" His voice was compassionate and gentle, warm and inviting despite the tender, wounded pride. His tone stopped her. She wrestled with her emotions, wanted to trust his devotion, to welcome his offer, to belong. At the same time, she wanted to escape, to put distance between herself and any man. Tate's hand on her shoulder compelled Tana to turn toward him. "I'm sorry, baby." His hand slid down her arm, and he took her hands in his. "I don't want to move too fast for you. If I need to slow down, just say so. I promise you can be honest with me." Despite her willing it not to, she felt the sting of a tear slide from her eye and down her cheek, followed by the soft brush of his fingers.

She started back toward the kitchen and out of his reach. "I can't ask you to wait for me, Tate. It's not fair to you."

Not prepared to let her go, Tate followed. In one smooth motion, he turned her fully to him, cupped her face in his hands, and allowed her sea-green eyes to swallow him. "Even if I have to wait for the rest of my life, you are worth such a wait."

"Tate Palmer, you've known me for what, six months? Nine months?"

"A year."

"A year," Tana repeated softly, shocked at the length of time. She pulled herself away from him again and pushed on with her point. "How can you say that? You don't really know me." Once again, she could feel the pain in his eyes. Tana hated herself for hurting him like that, and yet she was sure if she allowed him much closer, he would hurt her. Leave her. Run from her. If he knew her, he would feel differently. Better to hurt than to be hurt, she tried to convince herself. Yet something deep within Tana questioned the wisdom of her thoughts.

"You know what?" That grin eased across his face. "I'm hungry. Can we talk about this later?" Tana was grateful for the open door and handed him a plate.

Chapter 2

Georgia, 2001

Once again, Millie found herself sitting in a federal prison visitor's booth on one side of a glass window, waiting for his arrival on the other. How had it been four years of this? Because of this man, Jack. Good heavens, would this ever get easier? Millie struggled to not lose herself in self-pity. "Jesus, give me the grace to do this," she silently prayed.

Words and conversations tumbled throughout her head. Four years of them. The first visit was so short—she cried longer in the parking lot afterward than she was in the room with him. Four years had begun to soften him; he would now greet her with a smile. Yes, she thought the hard edge was rounding and softening. "Holy Spirit, be the comforter and counselor. Mine and his. Guide me, but keep me out of the way."

A tap at the window broke her thoughts. She looked up and forced herself to smile at him. Millie picked up the receiver to hear his voice, "Mrs. Jensen."

"Jack." She waited for him to take his seat across from her. Taking a deep breath, she looked him in the eyes and prayed for her words to be true. To hit their mark. To change both of their futures. To lead them both to the path of righteousness. "Jack, I forgive you."

"Mrs. Jensen, I don't deserve it. I can't tell you where your daughter is now." Millie caught her breath at the mention of Montana; she hoped Jack didn't notice. He didn't seem to, as he continued talking, "Eight years ago, I did some pretty evil things, and I deserve to sit in this place. I cannot accept forgiveness."

Millie let the words come. "No, Jack. None of us deserve forgiveness. But that's why we need it—because we don't deserve it. It's a gift. Wherever my daughter is does not change the gift I'm offering to you. Anyway, it's not mine to give. I've been given the same gift of forgiveness and must give what I've been given. What you do with it is your choice."

Jack sat silent as he puzzled over her words. His choice? How could he choose what to do with it when he didn't even understand it?

Millie watched as Jack turned the words over in his mind, not knowing his thoughts but understanding the feelings. Softly she spoke again, "Let me put it this way. Imagine you are walking a deserted road through a forest. The tree covering is thick, making the air cool and damp. You have been lost in the forest for days, which makes the road a welcome sight. However, after hours of walking its edge, no cars have driven by. Every so often, as you walk, the sun breaks through the tree cover. Those bright spots are the light by which you see and provide the warmth that keeps your body moving. That light is a gift. You can choose to walk in it, gaining the warmth and light, or you can walk around it. That is what I mean by forgiveness being a gift. It's there, like the sunshine, but you do not have to get in it. If you do, you will be warmer, but you can choose to stay cold."

Washington, DC, 1991

Once John was satisfied that Carleigh had walked into her job at the District Attorney's Office, he turned the car to go to his office. As he drove, he allowed his mind to think, to wander back to that night some more. His thoughts tumbled over each other in his head. They settled on the conversation with Carleigh as they had walked to her condo from the bar.

"Why are you so agitated tonight, John?" Carleigh had her arm in his as they strolled the brisk ten-block walk. The calendar may have said spring, but the local weather hadn't received the memo. The night air chilled her skin to match John's mood.

"I hate when they start messing with each other."

"It's all good-natured."

"Is it? It always seems to me like they push that edge a bit much. I mean, I thought they were going to start throwing punches in class the other day." John slowed his walk and turned to face her. "Can I be honest?"

"Of course."

"I've made some decisions Lee isn't going to be happy with . . . and I guess that has me worked up a bit."

"Decisions? Like what?"

"Like money. To support a wife and family, I need to make more money than working for the prosecution. Which means I will be taking Belmont up on his offer."

"Oh, John!" Carleigh's disgust was palpable. "You know I love Belmont . . . I mean, he's your family. But . . ." She trailed off a bit as she considered her wording. "I'm glad he's only a cousin and not closer. It's just not worth getting into bed with that snake!"

"Come on; he's not that bad—"

"Not that bad?" Carleigh rolled her eyes, "He's like fingernails on the chalkboard of my soul. I mean, he's fun to hang around with some, but I can only take small doses." Her voice descended to a near whisper, then crescendoed as her frustration grew. "Not that bad? He's a viper, and you know it. You cannot trust that man, John!"

"Hey, Fireball, settle down!"

"John Palmer, you know I love you." John thought maybe the edge in her voice had softened. "But I cannot support that decision. I won't be bound to him." In the quiet of her hesitation, John could almost feel her fear. When she spoke again, it was barely audible, "If you work for him, I can't be bound to you either." He pulled her into his arms and kissed her mouth before she got another word out.

"Okay, you win," he whispered. Carleigh pulled back far enough to see his eyes, and he reached up to brush a few red strands away from hers. "I'll work with Lee, and if we stay broke forever, so be it." Carleigh laughed at his dramatics and leaned in to kiss him again.

"Two lawyers can't really be broke, can they?"

"I'm sure there's a lawyer joke there somewhere," he replied, grateful to see her laughing with him.

As he walked into the office, the phone in his pocket buzzed him back to reality. He fished it out to look at the number and winced a bit. Stepping back into the hallway, he swiped the answer button. "I told you not to call me. Yes, I'll get the money . . . No . . . No. I'll figure it out. Soon. I will . . . Belmont, I . . . I told you I will. . . . Fine. Later." He ended the call and took a deep breath. Not really the way he wanted to start his day.

Los Angeles, 2016

Stan met them at the studio office door, "Hey, champ! Thanks for coming today. I have several people I want you to meet." He held the door open for Greg and Silvia, "Come on in! Everyone is excited you are here."

"Thank you," Silvia answered as they stepped through the door. Stan shut it behind them, gave Silvia a knowing smile, and knelt to look Greg in the eyes.

"Nervous?" Greg could only nod his head, which made Stan smile again. "This is a great look. Are you a Dodgers fan?"

"Not really," he answered shyly.

"Greg," his mother corrected, but Stan just laughed.

"He's honest. I like that," he told Silvia with a wink. Stan turned back to Greg and asked, "Who do you like?"

Greg didn't have to think long. With a grin as bright as the sparkle in his eyes, he answered, "Peyton Manning is my favorite, but he retired. I like to watch Russell Wilson now."

"Ah, a football guy. I like that. Now, wait a minute . . . didn't Russell beat Peyton in the Super Bowl?"

"Don't get him started," Silvia laughed.

"That's why I like him now. Anyone who can beat Peyton like that has got to be a good player, right?"

"That's a fact, Greg." Stan stood back up and ushered them down the hall. "Come on this way. I've got some people who would like to talk with you."

Washington, DC, 2018

"Derby wants us to meet with his team next week to depose the senator in the Blakely case," Tate told her between bites. "Remind me so we can look at our calendars. I want to get it on his schedule for early in the week if you can."

Smiling at him, Tana replied, "I'm pretty sure Tuesday afternoon will work for me. Is Senator West still in denial about the events surrounding his arrest?"

"Swimming in denial, despite all of the emails and video."

"And his son?"

"I think they are doing the backstroke together." Tate smiled as he tried to keep the dinner conversation light by turning from work-related topics to delighting Tana with tales of playful childhood antics. His lightheartedness always amazed her, despite the hardships he grew up under. And this man could get himself into craziness faster than anyone she knew.

After dinner, Tana and Tate rinsed the dishes and placed them in the dishwasher. Her mind buzzed with a million things she wished she could tell him, but fear kept her from opening her mouth.

She studied his face. That soft grin almost never left his lips, and the light that danced brightly in his eyes was stunning. And when she caught him looking at her, Tana thought that, somehow, that light shined even brighter. She watched those hands, so big, and yet with a tenderness in his touch that was almost more than she could bear.

"Hey, beautiful?" Tana looked up to see Tate had stopped, glass still in hand. "Where are you?"

"Just thinking, charming, I guess." She smiled back at him.

"Oh? Care to share?" he finished putting the last glass into the dishwasher.

"I was thinking how nice it would have been to know the little boy you were."

"Ha! Guess you'll have to be satisfied with knowing the little boy I am." Again she giggled at him. He always did that to her, and somehow she found it both refreshing and comforting. Tate shut the dishwasher door, turned back to her, and once again gathered her up in his arms. Tana thought he was one of less than half a dozen men she had ever allowed to touch her like this. Tate topped a list that included her father, Uncle Paul, and Uncle Troy. Tate held her close as if he would never let her go, and if she was honest, she didn't want him to ever stop.

"I didn't answer your question," he whispered into her ear.

"What question?"

"How I know . . ." Tana pulled back from his arms but held onto his hands to get a better look at his face. He smiled again, "Go sit down, and I'll bring you some coffee." She hesitated to let go of his hand. "Go on, I'll be right there."

Tana moved to the living room, where she sunk into her usual spot on the couch. The sounds and scents of coffee preparation wafted toward her. Thoughts and images wandered and drifted through her mind again, her fingers tracing the decades-old scar, like following a dark, bumpy road. With little effort, she could still feel the blade pressed against her cheek, the bite as it drew blood. If she tried, the pungent stench of the alcohol on his breath would overpower the fresh brew fragrance in her living room.

Tate came from the kitchen carrying two big mugs. In one motion, he set them on the table in front of her and pulled her back into the moment. "Thank you, charming."

"You are welcome, beautiful." His grin was infectious. Tate sat beside her but did not crowd her. She was ever so grateful for how he could be so sensitive to her personal space. "So let me tell you what I do know."

Tana could feel her heart pound and was sure if he looked, Tate could see it try to escape her chest. "I know those sea-green eyes are going to drown me every time I look into them. I know that dark hair is calling my fingers to play. I know I want with everything in my being to kiss that mouth of yours. I know you are the sweetest, smartest, most challenging woman I know." He reached toward her face. His fingers almost danced as they traced the scarred jawline. "I know you had an unbelievably horrible experience. I know, God willing, I will never allow anything to wound you again. And I know I want to spend the rest of my life both protecting you and rectifying your pain."

"But you don't even know what that is. Or how much it will cost you." The tears she fought so hard against crested the edge of her lashes and made their way down her cheeks.

"I don't care the cost; I'll pay." He studied her face, drinking in her eyes a little more. "I am not playing with you. I am not that kind of man." Again Tate moved closer and took her face in his hands. "I need you to understand the gift you are to me."

Tana turned her head away from him, "Some gift—a broken, useless toy."

"Stop, Montana." He did not raise his voice, but his tone was firm. "I will not stand for you to talk that way about yourself." He took a breath and allowed it to soften him, "My love, I know some men have treated you like that. I am not one of those men. I understand the true value you are. I need you to understand I am now and forever completely in love with you."

The words were both comforting and frightening. "Tate," her voice was almost lost in the silence of the room, "how can you be willing to attach yourself to me? To someone who does not have the ability to return that attachment? I feel I have no ability to trust anyone wholly."

"Because I am willing to walk whatever road we need to, for you to be able to begin to trust me. I understand loss and love. Losing my parents when I was pretty little was hard. But my Uncle Lee and Aunt Sonja stepped in and taught me love." He paused, making sure he had her full attention. "Together, they helped me not feel that wound so intensely. To not be afraid of the emptiness and feel like I was utterly lost. I want to help you in the same manner. I want to help you see how amazing you are. I am not afraid of a future with you. I am afraid of one without you. Honestly, I feel just talking with me like this, here, tonight, this is trust. You are trusting me with what I imagine is just a small part of the pain you carry. I will try to be trustworthy so when you feel comfortable, you can place even more trust in me. And if it takes a lifetime for you to be that comfortable with the concept, then I will wait. I will love you. I will walk with you."

Georgia, 2001

Jack made his way back to his cell, but his mind was a million miles from this place. For four years they had been having these conversations. This woman. This impossible, unbelievable, frustrating, amazing woman. He shook his head at his thoughts. He had turned this woman's entire world upside down, demolishing it. He could see the devastating destruction all over her face every time he looked at her.

He remembered that warm Georgia day. If he closed his eyes, he could see them. The delightful, loving, charming interaction between mother, father, and daughter—wife and husband. The woman was beautiful. The little girl, so sweet and innocent. They seemed an ideal family. Everything his was not. Everything he was not. Thoughts of his young son growing up fatherless tried to creep into his mind, but he pushed them aside. He had attempted to destroy the Jensen family as he had destroyed his own. And yet. Here she was, like a blade of struggling grass coming up out of the ashes of a devastating fire. Visiting him, more so than his own family, or what was left of his family, had. Crazy woman. She stirred his soul. For the last four years. And it was getting harder to shake it off.

Washington, DC, 1991

Hearing a knock on his door frame, John looked up over his computer screen. "Hi, Lee. What's up?"

"Can I talk to you for a couple of minutes?"

"Sure."

Lee stepped in and pushed the door shut behind him. He sat in the chair opposite his brother. They may be twins, but they were different in almost every way possible. Lee took a deep breath, "What happened in court the other day?"

"Belmont and Derby presented a more convincing case, I guess." He looked into the unblinking face of his brother, in the heavy silence between them. "What are you after?"

"I just want to know why you are struggling so much with them right now? We've been at this for several years now, but our convictions seem to be fewer than they were in past years. I don't like putting those people back on the streets, John."

"I know you don't. Neither do I, Lee." John studied his brother then tilted his head a bit to the left. "You accusing me of something?"

"No, John. I am just trying to figure out how that guy walked. It was a clear conviction, and somehow, he walked." Lee watched John for a bit then grinned at his brother. "Tell you what. You look like you need some time out with your wife. And I know an aunt who would love some time with her favorite nephew. Bring him over tonight; we'll watch him, and you and Carleigh get some dinner. Clear your head. Let's start fresh tomorrow."

The idea was as startling as cold water thrown in John's face. Dinner? Alone with Carleigh? Would she even want to go with him? They seemed to fight more than not as of late. Ever since . . . John sighed out loud. "I will ask her. Let's plan on it. Thanks."

Georgia, 2001

Millie pointed the silver MDX homeward. *Jesus,* she wondered, *why am I here? Am I doing any good? You promise beauty for ashes . . . where is mine? I've seen you do amazing things for other people. I know you are a good Father, but I've got to tell you, I'm struggling here. I can't see that you want to be good to me.*

"Father, my heart is grateful for the writers of the Psalms. And Job. For examples of people who were not afraid to be bold with you. And I'm grateful for a God who is not afraid of me being bold either."

She talked as she drove home, and her anger ebbed and flowed like ocean waves crashing against the shore. Every drive home from visiting Jack was like this. Oh, how she wanted to forgive and move on. Yet every new day found her still missing a huge chunk of her heart. Every day, she struggled with how to survive without that massive amount of a vital organ. *If he would just break a little more, Jesus. If Jack would just hear you . . . Maybe that's the problem; I haven't gotten out of the way enough for him to hear You talking to him. Show me truth.*

Chapter 3

Chicago, 2001

A few days later, the little girl was more alert, eating better, but no more communicative. The only time there was any life in her eyes was the brief moment Doorway Man came in to visit. He asked some questions, took some pictures, and promised to return once more. Even then, she did not utter a word. Blank eyes watched his movements. Most of his questions were unanswered, though he did receive one or two nods.

When Ms. Mitch visited, she brought gifts for the girl, including a coloring book, some crayons, and balloons. She set her keys, the book, and crayons down on the tray while she tied the small balloon bouquet to the table leg. There was a spark in the little girl's eyes then, too, as she appeared to find some comfort in this prize. At first, the book and crayons lay on her table untouched. However, when Michelle turned to pour the girl some water, the great treasure had disappeared under her pillow. It was as though she was afraid they would be taken away when she wasn't looking. Her eyes stayed fixed on the balloons. Still, the only spoken words in the room were Michelle's.

The sudden voice from behind her startled Michelle. "Hey, Michelle, can I have a word with you?"

Michelle turned to the nurse standing in the doorway, "Of course. I'll be right there." Facing the child, again, she told her, "I'll be right back, sweetie." Then she followed the nurse down the hallway to the desk.

"What's up, Susan?"

"I have the dietician here for a consult but no family yet. I thought maybe since you and Paul seem so interested in the girl . . ." She let her words hang in the air.

"I'm happy to meet with the nutritionist, but an agent is tracking her parents down right now. We hope to have them here within forty-eight hours."

"Oh, that's excellent news. I'll let the dietician know she can come back later to talk to the parents."

"Has she seen the girl already?"

"Yes, this morning."

"Perfect. Thanks, Susan." Michelle headed back into the girl's room. The child lay in the same place as if she hadn't moved a muscle, her keys still on the tray. Still, there was a noticeable difference in the room. "Awww. What happened here?" she wondered aloud but received no explanation for the balloons now shredded, hanging limply by the string, as if they had all popped.

Washington, DC, 2018

Tana tucked herself into bed and allowed her mind to wander through the evening's conversation. Like a river meanders through the mountains, Tana's thought trail rambled through the years and landed her back in college.

She had grown so much, and yet so little during those four years. She had made some friends, but no one genuinely knew her. Professors cultivated the growth of her mind, but her heart remained rocky and hard. She was so guarded that most other students quickly stopped trying to befriend her. Every relationship was surface-level, friendly but standoffish. Her roommate, an art major from California, was not in the room much, which seemed to suit both well. Well enough, they roomed all four years together. Theirs was a comfortable, loose, and non-threatening relationship.

Time with Tate had been astonishing. She couldn't remember ever feeling so secure and comfortable with anyone else. The way he engaged when she would talk to him about little things, she knew he listened. When Tate looked at her, when his eyes connected with her own, she knew he saw her. And each time their eyes met, she felt the cracking and crumbling of her inner walls. It was at once a terrifying and exhilarating feeling. The knowing and acceptance, feeling so valued, it was all almost overwhelming.

To be rejected for the things beyond her control was much too painful even to consider. The reality of that rejection was so drilled into her head, she wasn't sure she could ever believe anyone would just accept her. Or could accept her for who she was, if they knew. In her heart of hearts, she knew for the relationship to grow with Tate, she would have to take that step, risk the rejection. She thought about how she could discover his opinions of sunsets as her mind drifted off to sleep.

Los Angeles, 2016

Making his way home from school, Greg walked with his friends as far as each of their blocks. His house was still another three blocks away. "Hey, did you set your DVR? *Dr. Who* is on tonight," he asked Zack before they went their separate ways.

"Duh, it's always set. I think the doctor is fighting the Daleks on tonight's episode."

"Yeah, I love when he does that," Greg smiled at his friend. "Exterminate! Exterminate!" Both boys broke out into laughter before Greg added, "I'll see you tomorrow."

"Catch ya later," Zack called on the way to the door.

Greg continued walking the last three blocks alone. As he grew closer to his house, he noticed another car behind his mom's. Greg was nearly at the walkway before he realized whose car it was. The front door swung open as he turned into the driveway.

"There he is!"

"Hi, Mr. Stan."

Stan turned to Silvia and smiled, then turned back to Greg. "Guess what, buddy?"

"What?"

"Aww, no guesses?" Stan pretended to pout.

"Did I get it?"

"Winner! Winner! Chicken Dinner!" Stan grinned at the boy. "Yes! You got the part! Come on, let's go get some ice cream to celebrate."

Greg looked at his mom, "Can I go?"

"Why are you asking her? We're all going," Stan smiled.

"I guess we are all going," Silvia smiled back. "Let me get my purse and keys."

Georgia, 2001

The FBI agent walked up the long walkway, toward the large southern home, for what he figured would probably be the last time. He was feeling pretty good. The approaching conversation was the reason he had gotten into this crazy, nasty business. Conveying good news was so much better, though happened less often, than the bad news he tended to deliver.

He reached the door, straightened his jacket and tie, and as he rapped his knuckles on the old wooden door, he noticed the cracks in the paint. The door was weathered and aged, much as the Jensens had been from this nightmare they were living.

Millie had been home long enough to fix a cup of fresh mint tea and find her spot in front of the large window facing the back of the house. The knock on the door jarred the dancing thoughts in her mind, and they disappeared like trailing smoke. Millie slowly made her way to the front door.

Again, the thought crossed his mind that the last eight years had aged the woman. More than they should have. But then, losing a child always had that effect on parents. "Mrs. Jensen," he smiled at her. "May I have a word with you and Mr. Jensen?"

"Agent Roberts . . . come in. Let me find my husband. Would you care for a cup of coffee or tea?"

"Coffee would be fantastic—thank you."

"I'll be right back with it. Please, have a seat at the table. I will find Dave."

Once they were all seated, hot drinks steaming in front of them, Agent Troy Roberts pulled a photo from his folder. "Two weeks ago, some information came to light. As we began to follow it, things fell into place. Last week, the FBI put a plan together. Through that plan, they broke up a human trafficking ring in Chicago two days ago. There were several arrests made, though the leaders are still at large. This is why the media has been quiet about the arrests. This photo was sent to me by a buddy from that office. Would you please take a look?" He handed a black and white 5x7 of the face of a little girl in a hospital bed to the couple. Mrs. Jensen's gasp nearly cleared the room of oxygen; Troy knew it was on target.

"Montana Grace," the name was almost sticky in Millie's suddenly dry mouth.

Not wanting to bring his wife any unnecessary pain or unwarranted hope, Mr. Jensen questioned, "Are you sure? It's been eight years."

"I'm told she has the same birthmark on her chest."

They were on their way to Chicago within two hours.

Washington, DC, 1991

Driving home, John pondered Lee's conversation and his suggestion. Maybe getting out with Carleigh without the baby would be a good idea. Having a two-year-old was tough, and John couldn't remember a night out, just the two of them, in the two years since Tate was born. If nothing else, it would give him time to talk to her about her morning stops and the texts he had seen. He had tried once about six months ago to speak to her, but Tate had started crying, and that had put an end to the conversation. Frustrated, John had walked to the bar that night. He figured he would run into Lee. However, Belmont found him instead and talked him into playing poker with some guys John didn't know. When he returned home, his wallet at least a grand lighter, he was too drunk to remember what he had wanted to say in a conversation, and Carleigh was asleep anyway.

As he pulled into the driveway, John caught the site of Carleigh and Tate playing near the window. Mesmerized, he sat in his car and watched. The longer John sat, the more he wrestled the swell of emotions coursing through his body. He was angry about the things going on in their relationship and filled with awe and love for his family. Shoving his resentment aside, John turned the engine off and got out of the car. He walked toward the house when Tate spotted him from the window. John smiled at the way the boy's face lit up like a Christmas tree when they made eye contact. Tate ran to the door and greeted him with a sloppy, two-year-old kiss.

Carrying his boy as he walked into the house, he found Carleigh had moved into the kitchen and was pulling bell peppers from the fridge. "Hey, babe. How far are you on dinner preparation?"

"Hi!" she put the peppers down and kissed him, arms around both of her guys. "Just getting started."

"Fantastic. Stop." John laughed, and Carleigh tilted her head inquisitively. "Lee and Sonja want to watch Tate for us tonight and let us get out for a bit."

Tate repeated to John, "Wee, Nini?"

"Yeah, Buddy, Lee and Sonja."

"That's sweet, but I'm not ready to go anywhere, and Tate will be ready for bed soon."

"What's to be ready for? Come on. When was the last time we got to go anywhere?"

"Yeah?"

"Yeah, come on, just you and me." He kissed her again. Tate giggled and kissed his Momma's cheek at the same time. "Let's go to that little Italian place you love. It's not far from Lee's, and we don't have to be out too late."

"Okay, okay." She smiled at him, her eyes shining. "Let's do it!"

Chicago, 2001

Stepping out of the FBI building, something about Chicago felt cold to Millie. Or maybe it was something inside her that felt cold. Or numb. The emotions running through her heart and the thoughts in her head were overwhelming. Following Dave into the car, the conversation they just finished bounced around in her mind like a pinball.

She was on full tilt.

"Hey, Troy! Welcome to my town," the agent behind the desk jumped up to shake Troy's hand. Troy caught the offered hand and wrapped his left arm around Paul's back in a quick hug.

"Paul. It's great to see you. Becky's not happy she couldn't come to see you and Michelle." He turned to the couple standing slightly behind him. "Let me introduce you to Dave and Millie Jensen. Millie and Dave, Special Agent Paul Masters."

Once more, Paul held out his hand and smiled. "I'm so glad to meet you. I imagine you guys have lots of questions right now. I hope to be able to answer some. Please, sit down," he gestured to the seats in front of his desk.

"Thank you, Agent," Millie said as she sat in the chair.

"Please, Paul."

"Paul. I brought Tana's teddy bear. I was hoping to take it in when we go see her."

"I think that's an excellent idea."

"I also would like to pick up some flowers and balloons to take with us. Is there a good place for that before we get there?"

"Mrs. Jensen . . ."

"Millie."

"Millie. While I love your enthusiasm, I need to caution you on a couple of things. First, balloons do not seem to go over well with her."

"Really? She always loved them as a child."

"I can assure you that has changed." He paused as if considering his words while the concept of what might have changed for her child began to soak in for Millie. "I can also assure you there are other changes. Not knowing her as a young child makes identifying all changes tough, but I would bet she talked—at least some?"

"Oh, yes, she was talking more than the average child by eighteen months."

He sighed. "She has not spoken a word in the forty-eight hours we've had her. To anyone."

Chapter 4

Montana stood, studying her reflection in the mirror. Most women would be thrilled to see such features staring back at them. Average height, slim build. Somehow, Tana knew the face in the mirror was a striking one, but all she saw was the dirty little girl she felt in her heart.

It had been fifteen years since she escaped from that dark hole, and yet in her mind, it could have been yesterday. The years had not washed away the feeling of those men's hands on her body, nor cleared her nose of their stench any more than it had washed the birthmark off her chest. Echoing through her mind, she heard the deep voices of the men telling her how her daddy did not want her anymore . . . how no man wanted her. Without much effort, she could still feel the cold around her, smell the nauseating air, hear every sound. Some things just don't leave a little girl's memory, even with the alcohol and drugs they force upon her.

Reverberating in fierce competition, Tate's voice, like soft symphonic notes, tried to drown out the squeal of an out-of-tune electric guitar, but his words told her something else. Something she couldn't remember anyone else ever telling her. Tana thought about their walks around the Tidal Basin and Jefferson Memorial. That first walk had been a captivating moment. Their conversation had been easy, and she was taken a bit off guard by it. As they walked, he talked, and she allowed herself to absorb the feelings his presence created.

Tana had been slowly walking around the cherry trees, studying each one, noting the difference between the varieties, when she caught sight of Tate watching her. He smiled. "You seem to be very comfortable here. It's almost like watching you dance with that tree. Very natural."

Tana was pretty sure she had blushed, and she quickly turned to the trees. "Did you know this one here, the Yoshino cherry, or Japanese flowering cherry, is about seventy percent of the trees here? And all the other types are twelve percent or less?"

The walk had led them to the back of the Memorial, and they were heading toward the Potomac.

"You know, I've lived in this area my whole life, but I don't think I've ever taken the time to learn about these trees. So no, I don't know the percentages." He grinned at her enthusiasm.

Tana laughed at herself. "I guess that's a tourist hazard. I've only been in DC for four years, so I'm still learning the area. This is a place I come often. I can be alone but not alone here."

She faced the trees lining the edge of the Potomac. "See the trees there? The weeping cherry trees?" She turned back and caught him looking at her, rather than to where she had pointed. Tana reached up and turned his head in the direction she had motioned. "Those. They are my favorite."

Tate smiled, turned back, and locked his eyes on Tana's. "They are very pretty. But, you? You are my favorite view."

At the moment, she felt both irritated and intrigued by his words. Even in the memory, her cheeks filled with color. When had a guy talked to her like that? Soft, gentle, inviting, and strong. Never. And yet, Tate often told her of the beauty he saw in her. Of his desire for her. Of his love for her. She could see the truth of his words in his eyes every time he looked at her. She could feel it in his touch. Still, somehow her heart wanted to reject it as fiction. Or at least write it off as a passing trend, a fad. Even a year later, she expected it to fade, waiting for him to turn on her, to show himself to be someone other than who he presented himself to be.

Which voice was trustworthy?

Tana let her mind wander to her parents. They had seemed thrilled when they found her. Despite all of the times she was told her father didn't want her, they treated her better than the other men had. They would tell her repeatedly how they loved her—and of their joy in her. They made it possible for her to go to college, to learn of a better life than what she'd experienced, and to find a purpose in helping other young girls escape the nightmare as she had.

Even these seventeen years later, she found it so much harder to believe she was wanted, than to believe she was worthless trash—even by them. Why did she have so much trouble believing her parents' words? Why was it easier to feel and accept betrayal than love?

As she studied the image in the mirror, she reflected on how college had been good for her. She laughed as memories of her professors flooded her mind. There was some life breathed into her there, though she still struggled to thoroughly understand some of the lessons they had taught. There was one professor who always told her how valuable she was—her beloved Kay Stoltenberg. *Valuable like a sunset,* she would say. Tana had trouble believing her words, but she tucked that nugget away for further contemplation. Kay, Tana determined, would probably like Tate.

And Tate. Sweet Tate. She often found herself wondering if he was too good to be true. If he knew half the truth, he'd probably see just how unworthy she was of his affections. She studied the jagged scar streaking just above her jawline again. Why did he not seem to see it? Why was he not bothered by it? How was he not ashamed and afraid of it, as so many who only walked by her seemed to be? She determined she would just have to tell him everything . . .

To build her courage, she picked up the phone and typed a few letters; various names scrolled by as she tapped the screen. If there was one way to get ahold of her emotions and piece this puzzle together, this was it. The ringing phone simultaneously eased her nerves and lit them up. Questions ebbed and flowed through her mind until a voice answered. "Hello, my favorite Sunset Aficionado!"

Tana grinned at the sound of her nickname. "Hi, Kay. Got a minute?"

Los Angeles, 2016

"You ready?"

Greg nodded as he looked at Stan, his eyes wide, as Stan tried to guess whether it was from fear or excitement. The line between the two seemed razor-thin. Stan just smiled and let out a little giggle as he reached out and tussled Greg's hair.

"You two have fun," Silvia called, digging through her purse for her keys. "Thanks again for taking him, Stan. I don't know how I would have done it and still kept my job."

"Hey, that's what I'm here for! I know traffic around here can be crazy. That's why we are leaving so early, even though he doesn't need to be there until 9:30." Stan winked at Greg and continued to reassure Silvia. "Don't worry about anything. I'll guide him through today, make sure he eats, and have him home by bedtime."

Shocked, Silvia stammered, "Bedtime? Really? Wow, I didn't realize he would be there that long." As an afterthought, she wondered out loud, "When will he get his homework done?"

Stan jerked back to face Greg, "Oh, that reminds me, Greg. Go get your backpack. You will have lots of downtime on the set to work with our tutor and make sure your homework is completed."

"Seriously? Oh, man," Greg grumbled as he headed down the stairs to his bedroom.

"And don't be slow. We need to make sure we are on time to the set."

Washington, DC, 1991

In the quiet of the night, Sonja Palmer took the time to sit on the couch. If it had been just her and Lee, she probably would have gone to bed. It had been a long couple of days, and the addition of the early morning Bible study she was attending made them longer. However, Lee had asked if she would be willing to watch Tate for John and Carleigh. Something about feeling like they needed some time to go out alone. *Sweet man*, she had thought. *How many guys look out for their brothers like that?* Never mind that it took him a couple of years to do it. Or that something must be affecting work for him to notice.

No, even still, that's pretty amazing that he would think about them getting time alone as a solution. So, of course, she had agreed. Now, a couple of hours past Tate's bedtime, she was beginning to wish they had gone to John and Carleigh's to watch him. At least the little man would be in his own bed, instead of in their guest room, and he wouldn't have to be moved once his parents came for him. She didn't mind them being out later; that probably meant they had really needed it. And she enjoyed the practice time for when she and Lee would one day have kids of their own. Such a sweet, joyful little boy.

It had taken Lee longer than John to propose, so they had only been married a few months, compared to the couple of years John and Carleigh had been together. John was rash and quick-moving, no matter what was at stake; Lee was more methodical, but when he made a decision, he was sure, and there was little that could move him from what he determined was the correct course of action.

Stretched out on the couch, Sonja found herself nodding off, and each time she awoke, it seemed a different show was on—or the same show in different moments—that insinuated she couldn't focus enough to keep up with whatever was going on, and she wasn't awake enough to figure it out.

This time, when she jolted awake, she wasn't sure if it was from the TV noise or something else. What was that? After about the third round, Sonja realized someone was knocking on her front door. Loudly. Goodness, did they want to wake the baby? Or the dead? "I'm coming; I'm coming!" Sonja called.

As she opened the door, she hurriedly asked, "Do you want to wake the baby? What time is it anyway?" Then she stopped at the sight before her, startled by the blue flashing lights and the two young men in uniform.

"I'm sorry, officers. I thought you were someone else. . . . Do you have the wrong house?"

"Ma'am, are you Sonja Palmer?"

"Yes, I am . . ."

"Is Mr. Palmer home?"

"Yes, he is, but he's asleep right now. He works in the morning. What can I do for you?"

"I'm Officer Phillips and this is Officer Shire. May we come in?"

"What is this regarding?"

Officer Shire took a bigger breath than Sonja expected. "Ma'am, do you know a John and Carleigh Palmer?"

"Of course." She paused as her thoughts caught up with the conversation. "Um . . . maybe I should go wake Lee. Please, come in."

Washington, DC, 2018

"So I need to tell you about this guy. . . . He seems to be a great guy. He has worked hard to get past my defenses and yet is not pushy or obtrusive. He's sweet and charming, and funny—"

"He sounds amazing," Dr. Stoltenberg agreed. "What's the struggle?"

"Ha! You know me well. Always a struggle," Tana sighed, trying to get her heart and head on the same page. "He is ready to be way more serious than I think I'm ready for. I mean, what if he's not the guy I think he is?"

"Let me tell you a story and see if that helps," Dr. Stoltenberg replied. "When I was a new professor, not much older than the students I was instructing, I heard a young evangelist. Dori was her name, I believe. Anyway, she gave the most beautiful sermon on mercy. We were in a small church, and it was a small crowd. . . . I think there were ten or fifteen of us there. She described mercy as being compassionate or kind toward an offender, an enemy—you know, someone under your power."

"You mean someone you have authority over?" Tana said, letting the idea sink in.

"You got it. The short of the sermon was the idea that mercy is to find honor in the very humanness of someone who does not act the same toward you.

"She went on to pose this question: 'Why would one do this? Try to find honor in someone not trying to find honor in you?' And honestly, we didn't have any good reasons to offer. We were young and brash and just wanted an eye for an eye—revenge, to let loose our anger on those who wronged us.

"But Dori, she began to talk about second and third chances. About loving others through our pain. About seeing the pain behind their actions and separating those actions from the human beings they were. She ended by asking us to think about two questions: First, where do I need to show mercy? The answer to that is, I need to show mercy to the people I tend to judge. And second, where in my life do I need to receive mercy? That would be the area I need help and understanding in.

"See, to show mercy, you have to understand mercy. You have to be shown mercy. Because if you don't see mercy, you can't believe that such compassion exists. I think this young man is showing you mercy that you don't fully understand because you've never seen it before. Because you've never seen it, you can't believe it is real."

"Wouldn't my parents looking for me be a form of mercy?"

"Do you see that as mercy or the love of parents?"

"Is there a difference?"

"Oh, I think so. A person can choose to have mercy or not. Most parents cannot choose to love the child they brought into this world. It is part of their DNA, if you will."

"Let's say you are right; I've never seen mercy like that from people and have only seen the love of my parents. If that's the case, how do I go about trusting that reality?"

"Ah, isn't that the million-dollar question? If you're asking what I believe, I believe you have to take a leap of faith. Dive into the water, so to speak."

Los Angeles, 2016

Stan steered the car onto the busy 101, heading into Hollywood. At this time of day, the fifteen-mile drive should take them a good forty-five minutes. Maybe more. Good thing Greg didn't have to be there until 9:30. They should arrive with an extra forty-five minutes to walk him through a few aspects of the movie business. Stan stole a glance at the ten-year-old boy seated beside him. Such a sweet kid. Blond hair, blue eyes. The picture of innocence. Subconsciously, Stan ran his tongue over his lips and smiled. His deep voice broke the silence between them.

"Nervous?" Stan asked. Greg jumped at the sound, which made Stan laugh. "Sorry, buddy, I didn't realize you were so far in thought. Whatcha thinkin' about?"

Smiling shyly, Greg looked at the older man. "I just hope I can do well enough to make my mom proud."

The idea made Stan smile. "You two are pretty close, huh?"

Nodding, Greg quietly answered as he turned back to look out the window. "Yeah." Stan could tell there was more behind the answer and waited. It didn't take the boy long to continue. "Since Dad died, she's all I have."

"Oh, I'm sorry. I didn't know; I just assumed she was divorced. What happened?"

"Yeah, that's what most people think." Greg wavered and swallowed as if trying to keep his emotions in check. A light sigh escaped his lips before he added, "And it's easier just to let people think that. It's still hard for her to talk about Dad."

"I'm sure. It's got to be hard to lose someone you are that close to."

"Yeah, she doesn't talk about it much to me, but I know she thinks she could have done something to stop it. I mean, they had been fighting."

"Fighting?"

"Uh-huh. Money's always been an issue. I don't even know what the actual fight was about—bills probably. That's why he left that night, to cool down from the fight."

"Your mom told you all of that?"

"Well, I could hear a lot of the yelling, but I couldn't tell you for sure what was said. Later, Mom said she should have stopped pushing, and maybe he wouldn't have left."

"Pushing for what?"

"She wanted to go back to school. Honestly, I think the idea scared him. He once told me he thought Mom was smarter than him, and when she found out, she'd leave him for someone else."

"He told you that?"

"Yeah." The boy paused, still looking out the car window, though Stan was pretty sure he was watching the drama in his head. Greg turned and managed a weak smile. "They both talked to me like I was their friend, and I'm not sure either knew the other did."

Chicago, 2001

When the Jensens arrived at the hospital, they felt prepared for what they would find. Special Agent Roberts and Special Agent Masters had spent considerable time discussing their daughter's condition with them. Together, the four of them had tried to map out a plan to aid the girl in her recovery. Dave Jensen was willing to spare no expense for Montana; she was their only child. Still, the first sight of her was shocking.

They stood outside the intensive care room watching her sleep, trying to gain some kind of control over their emotions, even if it wasn't real control. They wanted to be strong for her, to love her back to health, to not drive her farther into her shell.

When they finally walked into her room, they were as calm as they could manage. They carried in her favorite teddy bear, some flowers, and a few pieces of her favorite candy. The Jensens wore smiles on their faces, but their hearts broke all over again as they began to understand the depth of the damage done to their daughter.

"Montana Grace . . ." Millie Jensen called softly to her daughter. The girl did not even know her name anymore. Millie walked around to the side of the bed the girl faced. "Oh, my sweet baby girl. I have missed you so much." Millie reached down and brushed a strand of hair back from the little face, taking note of a scar she'd never seen before. Montana did not move. Millie continued anyway, "I am so grateful God has brought you home to me."

The girl's flat, empty eyes seemed to look right through Millie. There didn't seem to be much life left in them. In fact, there was no indication Montana knew her parents at all. When they placed the teddy bear beside her, Montana wrapped her little arms around it and held on tightly, without much of a glance their way. She didn't show any signs of recognition—but neither did she let go of it for the rest of the time she was in the hospital.

After spending about thirty minutes with her daughter, Millie excused herself and left the room. She made her way to the hospital's chapel, stumbled down the aisle, flung herself on the altar, and wept bitterly.

Washington, DC, 2018

Tana picked up her phone at least a dozen times and put it back down at least a dozen times. She never thought one call could be so difficult. Her head believed Tate when he said it didn't matter. Her heart was afraid he would not be able to even look at her when she finished. Afraid he would see how dirty she really was.

The vibration in her hand startled her. Maybe that's what she wanted, for him to force her hand by calling first. She let it ring again, trying to gather her nerve. Taking a deep breath, she pressed the button, "Good morning, charming."

"Good morning, beautiful." He spoke with the cheerfulness of a bluebird's song, much too enthusiastic for so early in the morning.

Inside, Montana cringed a little. Oblivious, Tate continued, "How did you sleep?"

Ignoring the zeal in his voice, she answered honestly, "Not so well."

"Oh? You know I don't like to hear that."

"I want to talk to you. I—I need to talk to you."

"So talk, my love, the computer geeks have my computer for the day, so I'm all yours as long as you need me."

"No, not on the phone. I want to speak to you face to face."

"Done. When and where?"

"How soon can you be here?"

Chapter 5

Washington, DC, 2018

Thirty minutes.

Tate called the office and told them he would be late. He didn't have much of a caseload anyway, and since he was waiting on the tech department to figure out what was going on with his computer, Tate couldn't do much in the office anyway. He made the trip in thirty minutes. As he approached Tana's door, he took a deep breath of his own. He was pretty sure they had ended well last night and so felt unsure about her desperation this morning. Possible reasons she might want to talk to him swam through his drifting mind until the coffee he held in his hands splashed onto his jeans. "Oh, man," he blurted before he continued his walk to her door, which Tana opened before he could even knock. "Wow, you are on the ball this morning, beautiful."

She giggled a little at him. "Charming, I can hear your car coming three blocks away."

"Ah, a giggle followed by a snappy comment; that's good, right?" Tate heard the door shut behind him as he set the two coffee mugs down. "Either way, it is a better direction for me since I've already spilled the coffee."

"Are you nervous?" She watched him grab a kitchen towel for his jeans before he turned to face her and stood silent for a bit.

"Are you going to tell me you never want to see me again?" He finally asked, the towel hanging from his hand.

"Ummm, not this morning."

"Then, nope, not nervous a bit." There was that infectious grin again. He set the towel on the table, reached out to her, and she allowed him to pull her in tight. Tana felt her body begin to relax once more.

"I want to talk to you about some rather harsh things, though. And yes, before you ask," Tana tried to smile back at him, "I am rather nervous." As Tana sat on the couch, Tate grabbed the coffee and handed one to her as he sat beside her. "Outside of some counseling, and maybe a professor, I've never actually talked about any of this."

"No other guys? No girlfriends?

"I have never trusted guys, other than my uncles and Dad, who all know, and we just don't talk about it. I never wanted them to have to deal with the reality of the details. Other guys have never been around more than a couple of weeks. They sure never got close enough to hold my hand or hug me the way you do. The very fact that I am even talking to you is so weird for me.

"And I don't have many deep conversations with other women. This is not the kind of thing you chat about over coffee at the local coffee shop. The 'deep' conversations I've had have always been philosophical, never personal."

Tate took in all Tana said before quietly responding, "If you are sure you are ready . . . I don't want you to feel pressured at all."

"I know you don't, Tate," Tana insisted, fidgeting with the fringe of her cut-off jean shorts. "And that attitude is why I feel like I need to now. I want you to understand what you might be getting yourself into." She took a deep breath, her eyes staring at the floor, willing her nerves to be still. She lifted her head, her eyes settling on an image across the room. "You remember the picture with my aunt and uncles?" Tana pointed to a 5x7 on her bookshelf.

"The one taken when you graduated college? Sure."

"Well, they're not really my uncles or my aunt—not by blood anyway. They are FBI agents. Uncle Troy is actually Special Agent Troy Roberts, who started working with my parents the day I was kidnapped."

"Kidnapped? How scary for all of you."

Tana chuckled at the thought. "Yes, it was, but that was the easy part."

The idea visibly rocked Tate. "Easy?"

"If you can call it that, yes. See, Uncle Paul is actually Special Agent Paul Masters. Uncle Paul walked into my life the night they broke up the trafficking ring that had kidnapped me."

Tate exhaled as he felt his body melt into his chair under the weight of her confession. "Oh, Tana." His near-whispered apology went unheeded as Tana continued her story.

"He rescued me from the pit where they kept me. Aunt Michelle, Paul's wife, was the EMT who cared for me." Tana took another deep breath and looked up at Tate. She braced herself for the look of horror she expected to find. Or the look of shock. Or the look of disgust. What she did not expect to see was the tear that streaked his cheek.

"There's a lot of it I just don't remember. Even after years of counseling. They tell me when I was four, I begged my parents to see the circus. I wanted to see the animals. They gave in, and we went. We were having fun until my mom discovered I was no longer behind her. I had been holding her hand, but I let go when I saw a bunch of balloons as they blew away and ran after them. Mom says between my letting go of her hand and her turning to see what I was doing, the crowd swallowed me." Tana paused, took another deep breath, tried to gain her courage, then looked Tate in the eyes.

"I remember realizing I couldn't see Mom and a friendly man, with a goatee and a thick scar on his cheek, told me his name was Jack, and he would help me find my parents. Instead, he took me to the parking lot and tossed me into a van, and we were gone.

"The driver was not so friendly, and he kept telling me how my father told him he didn't want me anymore. I was a bad girl, and he was doing my father a favor by taking me off his hands. I can't remember how many times he backhanded me across my face. At one stop, he put a knife to my throat and told me if I didn't stop crying, he would stop me. Then he put a needle in my arm, and I stopped. I have no idea how long we drove; it seemed like forever. But my memory is also very hazy. The needles kept coming.

"When we arrived, the driver took me into a building and handed me over to another man. He informed me that he now owned me, that I must do whatever he said, or he would kill my family. He was basically my pimp. For years, he told me daily how worthless I was and that maybe I could win back my father's love if I treated this guy or that guy well. I really don't know when I quit believing him."

Washington, DC, 1991

The sound of little feet coming down the hall almost made Sonja sick. The moment she had dreaded since the officers left was approaching. How on earth do you tell a two-year-old? Telling an adult is next to impossible. But a baby? It will take him years to understand the depth of what just happened.

Soon after the arrival of Officers Shire and Phillips, Lee left with Shire to identify the bodies. If she was honest, Sonja was grateful for Tate sleeping in their guest room so she didn't have to go to the morgue. She had a run-in or two with the coroner, whose name she could never remember, with his wire-rimmed glasses and equally wiry build. Maybe it was the way he looked at her that made her feel like he wanted her on a slab in his freezer. She shuddered.

Even though she didn't go, she still didn't sleep much that night. In the early morning hours, when Lee returned home, neither of them slept much. Rather they lay in bed and cried together.

As soon as Tate rounded the corner into the kitchen, Sonja could feel the tears start fresh. Rolling from her eyes as her mind raced to find words. Any words. Tate looked at her, and some noise escaped his lips. "Nini? Choca milk? Momma?"

The sound of him trying to say her name made her tears fall harder. She scooped the little boy into her arms and held him close to her chest. "I'm so sorry, baby. I'm so, so sorry," was all she could manage. Lee walked over and encircled them both.

"Tate we have to tell you something, I'm not sure you're going to understand." Tate turned his face to his uncle. "Mommy and Daddy are not coming home. They died last night. You are going to come live with Aunt Nini and Uncle Lee."

Tate studied Lee's face, then asked his uncle the same thing he had asked his aunt, "Choca milk?"

Lee laughed a bit. "Oh, Nini . . . this is going to be a ride . . ." He kissed the top of his wife's head. Turning back to Tate, he said, "Yes, buddy, I'll get you some chocolate milk."

Los Angeles, 2016

"Cut!" The call from the director meant Greg was done for the morning, though it was still early. He moved from the set toward his backpack. Being done with the scene meant he needed to get some homework finished. "Hey, uh, Greg." The voice pulled him from his thoughts.

"Yes, sir?"

"Sir," the man grumbled under his breath. "You trying to make me feel old, boy?"

"No, si—uh. No," Greg stumbled through his answer. "Mom always said to be respectful and polite to everyone. She says, 'It's a respect thing, not an age thing.'"

Adding to Greg's confusion, the director ignored his explanation and simply commanded, "Come here a minute."

"Yes, si—uh. Okay." Quickly he moved closer to the director's chair, where the man still sat, flipping through pages for the next scene, his greying hair falling forward, hiding his face. Greg knew he wasn't scheduled to be in any other shots that day, and his mind raced to understand what he had done to warrant being singled out.

The man didn't even look up as Greg approached him, the pages in front of him clearly more interesting than Greg was. "How long you been working now?"

"Uh, a couple of weeks, I guess."

"You like it?"

"Yes."

"Good. You keeping up with your homework?"

"Yes," Greg felt his nerves fire up in the flush of his cheeks.

"Good." For the first time in the conversation, the director managed to take his eyes from the papers in his folder, flip his long bangs back from his face and actually look at Greg. A slow smile crept across his lips. "Good," he repeated himself. "I've got some people I want you to meet if you have some extra time this afternoon."

Washington, DC, 2018

"My handler, or pimp, made me call him Daddy," Tana continued telling Tate in detail about one child pornography session in which she was an unwilling participant. How men who paid large amounts of money for the use of a child abused her.

"When I was about eight, Daddy took another girl and me to a small hotel room. When we walked in, a guy was sitting at the little table sharpening a knife—I think mostly for effect so we would be more compliant. They stripped us of our clothes and began taking pictures of our naked bodies.

"Between shots, I moved the wrong way and knocked over a drink on the table, which spilled across the table and got the knives wet. In a fit of rage, he picked up a knife and cut my face.

"It's funny the things one remembers from an ordeal like that. Daddy was standing between the guy and me, and he had the habit of tying his shoelaces to the side of his foot instead of on top. I remember watching my blood splatter on his laces and thinking how odd it was the bow was not in the center of his foot, as my mom had taught me to tie mine. The images that stick in your mind . . ."

She laughed lightly, more of a brushing off of the memory than an actual laugh, followed by a sigh. "He reacted by beating the guy for his shoes. Then after looking at my face, told him it was no big deal, they were ready to move me anyway, that I was getting too old for most of his clients. So at that point, I learned I was worth less than a pair of shoes."

Tana then told Tate of the awful place they moved her to. She thought near some mine, where the men were rough, dirty, and broke. They paid a little money for a little time and just rotated out, anywhere from twenty to forty a day made their way to her room. Remembering those times, it was now her cheek that was wet.

Tana felt Tate's body move closer to hers, as he gathered her in his arms. Her head rested on his chest, and the grief she had held inside for so long flowed from her body in a sweet release.

Once her sobs had settled a bit, Tate leaned down and kissed the top of her head. "I want you to know," his voice was almost a whisper, "this changes nothing, Tana."

Tana sat up and stared at him. "How is that even possible? I have been used and tossed aside. I am broken."

"Because it is the past. Because despite all the garbage that surrounds you, I see the beauty you truly are. I am not the one who tossed you aside. I will never be that man. I want to be the one to help you heal."

Los Angeles, 2016

Stan caught up with Greg as he walked to the cafeteria. "Hey, big guy! Did the director talk to you?"

"Yeah," Greg smiled. "He said he has people he wants to introduce me to."

"Do you know who it is?" Greg shook his head, making Stan smile. "A few big names will be coming by in a couple of hours. One of them happens to be my dad."

"Is your dad an actor?"

The thought made Stan laugh. "No, buddy. My dad is a senator from New Hampshire. The big names are all in the government. I was telling Dad about you last night, and they all want to meet you."

Greg stopped short of the door. "Me?"

"Yes."

"Why me?"

Stopping in the doorway, Stan looked the boy over. Greg had a natural, athletic build, which spoke of confidence that wasn't as apparent when he talked. If he had to guess, the boy's need to please grew out of his lack of attention from his father. Stan could feel the blue in the boy's eyes pleading for affirmation. A smile formed on Stan's lips, and he reached out to tussle Greg's hair. "Because you are a great kid, and someday, you're going to be famous."

"Hey," Greg objected. "You're gonna get me in trouble with Rosie!"

Laughing, Stan agreed. "She does like to fuss over your hair, doesn't she?"

"Yeah. Even when I'm sitting, she says I'm gonna mess up what she did with it."

Stan chuckled at the image. "Come on, we need to get you some food!"

Washington, DC, 1991

The next few days were a blur as Sonja and Lee began the funeral arrangements, hosted visitors, and received a massive outpour of love and condolences. John and Lee's family was vast, including ten or fifteen cousins. Sonja had a hard time remembering; they were not usually around, except for weddings and, apparently, funerals. She'd met most of them at John and Carleigh's wedding, then again at her own wedding, and now, for the third time in four, almost five years. Sonja was both surprised and grateful when Belmont and Derby stepped in to help contact everyone and make many of the arrangements.

Even Belmont was a comfort to Lee. Since he had grown up with the boys, he seemed to be connected to them as if he were another brother. Funny. Thinking back to college, Sonja could not remember him acting so close to Lee then. It always seemed he was more in John's corner. But in the funeral home, Belmont would be there whenever Lee needed to talk. When Sonja walked into the kitchen area, where the family could rest and get something to eat, she saw Belmont sitting beside Lee, who had his head in his hands.

"I don't know why I feel like that," Lee was telling Belmont. Sonja made eye contact with Belmont, who just shrugged his shoulders in her direction. He moved his legs as if to stretch, noticing one shoelace had become untied. Absently, he moved to retie the laces, the bow resting sideways on his foot.

"I don't know either, Lee." Belmont spoke as he sat back up, reaching his hand to rest on his cousin's back. "Maybe it's some twin thing."

"What's that?" Sonja questioned Belmont.

Lee lifted his head; drying tears streaked his face. "Hi, babe."

"We were just discussing Lee's connection to John. He says he doesn't feel like John can be gone."

"I just can't believe it," Lee added.

Sonja knelt in front of her husband. "I know. This is going to be hardest on you. I am so sorry, my love."

Belmont stood and said off-handily, "You'll get past this. You'll see. Each day will get easier."

Shocked, Sonja corrected Belmont, "I'm not sure that's really an appropriate thing to say, Belmont." When he started to protest, she interrupted. "Oh, I know you mean well. However, Lee is grieving right now. Telling him he will get over the loss of his twin brother is at best inconsiderate." Belmont started to object again, thought better of it, and walked out of the room.

Carleigh's family was another story. As an only child, there weren't many relatives to contact. Sonja was able to get ahold of Carleigh's dad. She was afraid the news would kill him. He had lost his wife only two years before. He had made the trip from California to DC, but he looked much frailer than she remembered from when she'd last seen him at the wedding, and certainly a much different man from the one she knew from their college days.

Sonja wasn't even sure Carleigh's dad had seen Tate before this trip. Well, since he had been born anyway. She was pretty sure Carleigh's parents had visited right after he was born. However, her mom wasn't well even then, and they didn't stay long. Her mom passed away shortly after that. John, Carleigh, and the baby did travel to California for the funeral—if she remembered correctly. Sonja couldn't remember any other trip in either direction after that.

When the funeral was over, and everyone headed back to their own worlds, Carleigh's dad didn't stay long. As Sonja and Lee tried to settle into their new role as parents, she received a call that Carleigh's dad had passed away. She made a quick trip with Tate to attend the small funeral in California. After that, Sonja hoped and prayed there would be no more funerals for a long time.

Chapter 6

Georgia, 2001

aking his way down the hall, as he followed the aroma of coffee, Dave yawned and turned into the kitchen. Sitting at the table, coffee mug in hand, Millie watched out the window.

"Good morning," he sleepily murmured.

She didn't even look his way as she muttered her reply, "Good morning."

From behind the counter, Dave tried to spot the mysterious attraction holding her attention but could only see the trees in the yard. "Seeing some rare feathered friend?"

"Only the rare red-headed mute fledgling."

"Red-headed mute . . ." Dave stopped and repeated Millie's words, mentally visualizing a long list of known birds. "Nothing comes to mind. What does it look like?" He grabbed the mug and began to fill it with the liquid warmth from the glass pot.

"Oh, a little like you, and a little like me."

"Like you and me . . ." he repeated her once more before the words began to take hold. He let out a jolly laugh. "Montana is out in the tree?"

She set her cup down and turned to meet his gaze as he moved in her direction, grateful to see a full smile on his lips. "Yes, has been most of the morning."

Dave leaned over her shoulder, looking out the same window Millie had been. "In the red maple, huh?"

"Yeah," she nearly whispered.

He looked at his wife and then moved in to kiss her cheek. "She always did like that tree."

"So she did."

"What time is it?"

Millie turned to the stove, "Uh . . . looks like it's 9:30."

"Geez, why did you let me sleep so late? The mechanic is coming any moment," he set his cup down on the table, noting the puzzle in front of Millie. "Hey, you finished the border."

"Montana finished it," Millie answered, her attention back to the child making her way toward them. Dave reached out and lightly ran his fingers through the hair on the back of Millie's head.

"Like mother, like daughter?"

"Ha, yeah. I guess so." She looked back at him, her cheek resting in his palm for a moment. "Go get dressed. Otherwise, you'll be in your boxers when Joe comes to look at the tractor." He grinned and moved back to their bedroom.

Their backdoor opened slowly, and Montana timidly entered the kitchen. "Hi, sweet girl," Millie called to her. Montana smiled slightly and moved to the puzzle on the table. "Back for more pieces?" Watching as the child picked up two sections and snapped them both into place with little effort, Millie continued to talk to her with no response. "I've been looking for that one for the past thirty minutes, smarty."

"Dave?" a deep voice suddenly erupted throughout the house. Montana dropped to her knees and crawled under the table.

"Hey, Joe," Dave answered as he walked back into the kitchen, where he stopped, stunned to see his wife on the floor with his daughter. "Millie? What are you doing?"

"Hey, the door was open," Joe continued as he also entered the kitchen.

"Y'all go," Millie waved them off.

"What's going . . ." Joe started to ask, but Dave grabbed him and pulled him back into the living room, not stopping until the men were outside.

"Shh," Millie tried to soothe Montana, who sat hugging her knees to her chest, rocking ever so slightly. "It's okay, baby. Shhh. Shhh. Shhh."

The family spent the rest of that year working with females only: tutors, counselors, and doctors. The exceptions were when either Special Agents Roberts or Masters would drop by or when Montana's dad would be around. Somehow she seemed to know these three men meant her no harm. Montana trusted no one else.

Washington, DC, 2006

The years with Tate seemed to both fly and crawl. Sonja and Lee had taken the little insurance John and Carleigh left and set up an investment account for his college fund. It seemed the best use of the money as they tried to create a stable life for the boy. For the most part, he settled into living with his aunt and uncle like that was the place he had always belonged. Once in a while, though, Sonja grappled during the times Tate emotionally struggled with something. She always felt when he was hurting or acting out; they seemed to be the times he missed John and Carleigh the most.

It was during those times of struggle that she would find him sitting in his room looking through some old photo albums. Lee had wanted to get rid of everything. He said he felt like he was violating their privacy, though Sonja was certain that part of it was that the memories were too painful a reminder. She managed to keep a few things for Tate. She even had John and Carleigh's college sweatshirts made into pillows for the boy. And then there were the photo albums and a scrapbook Carleigh had put together highlighting Tate's first year. Her goal was to preserve anything that might help the boy feel connected to his parents.

One afternoon, when Tate was a junior in high school, Sonja started past his bedroom door and noticed him lounging on his bed, photo albums spread out in front of him. She stopped, laundry basket in hand. "Hey, buddy."

He didn't even look at her, "Hey . . ." His tone caught her off-guard. "You okay?"

"Do you think he looked like Uncle Lee?"

"Well." She walked into his room, set the basket down on his desk, and sat beside him. "He did when I first met the boys. But . . ." she smiled as the memories flooded her mind, "once you got to know them, you could see the differences." She pulled one of the albums onto her lap and flipped through a few pages. Finding a photo of Lee and John together, she stopped. "See?" She used her finger to trace their faces. "Notice how Lee's face is just a bit rounder than John's?" Tate nodded. "And though you can't see it as much in this picture, John's hair was always just a shade or two lighter than Lee's, much like yours."

Taking the book from her, Tate said wistfully, "I wonder how he would be different from Uncle Lee now."

Sonja stood and kissed the top of the boy's head. "I don't know, baby. . . . I miss them too." She picked up the laundry basket and started out of the room. His voice caused her to stop again.

"I've been thinking about college, Nini."

"Yeah?" She tried to keep her emotions level. The truth was, she had been thinking about the same topic. However, she was pretty sure their contemplations were very different. "What are your thoughts?"

"I think I want to go to Georgetown University and study law like the four of you did."

"Seriously?" Sonja tried to contain her excitement.

"Yes," he grinned.

"I think just knowing you have considered the possibility would make your parents proud. I know it makes your uncle and me proud." Sonja paused, wanting to make sure she worded her thoughts clearly. "It has to be what you want, though. What will make you happy?"

Tate slowly shook his head. "I like the idea I might be able to help someone out of the trouble they were in."

She smiled at him. "I think you would make an excellent lawyer."

Los Angeles, 2016

"Joey, I am very unhappy with your actions."

"But Mom . . ."

"No, don't. You've got to learn your actions have consequences."

"But Mom . . ."

"And consequences that don't mean anything—"

"But Mom—"

"Are worthless."

"But Mom . . ."

"Stop trying to interrupt me, son."

A booming male voice split the growing tension. "Maybe you should try listening to the boy, Helen."

"Cut!" The call echoed through the soundstage. Greg wondered if anyone yelled as loud as that man could. The man stepped out from the light barrier, making a beeline for the actress with long, quick strides. Tom Cochran. One of the greatest directors in all of Hollywood. Legendary for making hard-hitting movies and creating chaos on sets. Greg braced himself for the coming storm, yet found his tone even as he spoke, despite the hands flinging in Greg's direction. "Georgia, sweetheart, this is a child, not an untrained dog. He's been disobeying you, not peeing on the carpet. I want to see some passion. I want to feel your frustration with his actions." The imagery made Greg giggle.

"Really, Tom." she rolled her eyes at him. Georgia Collins grew up in front of cameras. She knew he wasn't questioning her acting. Stealing a quick glance Greg's way, she locked eyes on "Tom" to solidify her statement. "Dogs, I know. Kids, I do not." The announcement left Greg wondering if he should pee on her leg. The very idea made keeping a straight face impossible.

"Yeah? Then maybe you should treat him like he *has* been peeing on the carpet. Passion, Georgia! I want to see some passion!"

As the two discussed her ability—or inability—to act, movement off of the set caught Greg's attention, and his grin fell from his face. The lights in his eyes made it tough to see who all was on the other side of them. Over the last several weeks, Greg had grown more comfortable with the unknown faces just past the invisible barrier the lights created for his eyes.

However, today would be different. Today, Stan's dad was expected, and everyone was uptight. Knowing the adults on the set were excited about the visitors made Stan nervous. Or maybe it was the visitors that made Stan nervous. Either way, Greg could see it in his actions all morning, the way he ran his hands through his hair or picked at his fingers.

"You've got a great style, kid." That booming voice ripped into Greg's thoughts. It wasn't even that it was that loud, but rather that it was commanding, deep, gravelly, and strong. Greg spun back toward the set he had been standing on to see Wade Bale smiling at him. *The* Wade Bale. Talking to *him*. "It's fun to watch you work." Wade continued to talk, seemingly ignoring Greg's lack of entering the conversation. "I was so engrossed in your character, I nearly missed my cue."

The very idea of the great Wade Bale missing a cue because of him made Greg smile.

"Ah! A smile. That's great! You've got a great smile." Wade smiled back. "Keep it up, kid, and you'll go far in this business."

"Th-th-thank you, Mr. Bale." Greg stumbled over his own words, trying to pry them from his mouth.

"Hey, Greg!" The boy turned to see Stan jogging in his direction. "Hey! Come on, I have some people I want to introduce you to."

He turned his eyes back to Wade Bale as if to question leaving the presence of such greatness. Sensing the boy's reluctance, Wade reassured him, "Go on. We can chat later."

Georgia, 2018

"I read something yesterday. I've read it many times before, but I started pondering it more yesterday." Millie often found chatting more comfortable if they talked about something she had read.

"What was that?" Jack wasn't sure he cared; she was always talking about the Bible. Maybe, sometime, he'd read it so he could argue with her. Today wasn't that day.

"Romans 8:28. It says, 'And we know that in all things God works for the good of those who love Him, who have been called according to His purpose.' And I have to believe, when He says *all* things, He has to mean *all* things. Even this."

Jack listened to Millie's offering, yet again. His emotions teetered between obligation and disdain. He felt like this woman might never give up. What was it—twenty years he had been in here, and she had been coming to see him? He ran the dates through his head . . . twenty-one. Yeah, twenty-one years.

Jack grappled with his response. Had he begun to care about her? How did that happen? He looked up and caught her eyes. She smiled at him. How many people even grinned in his direction on any given day? Or throughout his lifetime?

A thought came to mind. Leigh. Millie reminded him of Leigh. That red-headed fireball, so fierce, strong, independent, and yet tender, nurturing, and supportive. She had been the only light in his world so long ago. He never knew he could miss someone as much as he missed Leigh. All these years and he still couldn't run from her. There was life in these two women he never understood. With Leigh, it drove him crazy, and he could feel the shame of his actions toward her flooding his whole body. With Millie, he wondered if maybe, somehow there were a second chance here.

"Are you okay, Jack?" Her voice pulled him back from the past into this moment.

"I thought of you yesterday." Jack changed the topic of conversation, attempting to steady the reeling he felt inside. Millie looked at him, puzzled, so he continued. "And maybe I should apologize for that thought. It came at lunch. They served some tofu slop. And I thought about you saying you actually like that stuff . . ."

"Ha-ha! Apology denied! Incidentally, I enjoyed a dish of tofu yesterday in a new Chinese restaurant nearby, cooked with black bean sauce and lots of fresh veggies and mushrooms, plus a bowl of rice, of course."

Even as she talked with him, Jack could feel the pain of the scars from his past. Every word she spoke reminded him of why he sat on this side of the table, and why this woman sat on the other side. He earned his way here; she was the sacrifice. And yet, for his whole life, he had acted like the world owed him something more, and she had been gracious and loving.

He was the debtor, and she honored him anyway. Struggling to control his emotions, Jack jumped up. "I've—I've got to go." And he turned away, almost running from her, hoping she didn't catch a glimpse of the tears he fought.

Millie sat at the table in stunned silence. Slowly she closed her mouth. *Jesus,* she silently prayed. *I'm sorry; I don't think I'm making a difference. Help me leave him in Your hands, that even this will bring You glory.*

Washington, DC, 2017

Tana eased her car into the open parking spot and took a deep breath. Going to court was the part of her job she most disliked. It was so much safer to sit behind her computer screen and work the guys on the other side. Honestly, she wasn't sure which was the obscure end. To tell them whatever they wanted to hear was easy—a trait she learned at a young age. She let them believe whatever they wanted was real and then snagged them in their filth. The less actual human contact she had, the better, as far as she was concerned. Tana took another deep breath to steel her will and managed to make her way to the front door of the courthouse. Once inside, the sound of her heels echoing in the empty halls felt as hollow as her heart.

On the docket today was low-level scum. Something about this guy reminded Tana of Jack. Maybe it was the kidnapping aspect or maybe the photography . . . she brushed the thought to the back of her mind. They had hoped to turn him on some of the higher-ups in this ring, but he was not working with them. Maybe some prison time would help with that.

As she walked into the courtroom, she glanced around the room. Lee Palmer, the prosecutor, sat at his table, scanning his notes. She had worked with him on several cases over the past few years, and there was something about his face that always felt sort of familiar to her. She figured he just had one of those faces—the kind that reminds you of someone, but you can never figure out who.

She turned her eyes to the defendant's table. How did this lowlife afford the Cooper, Street, and Irons law firm? One of the younger lawyers but still a heavy hitter. No wonder he didn't want to turn on his boss. She found a seat and listened to the testimony of an Officer Shire as she waited her turn.

Called to the stand by the prosecution, Tana's job was to tell the court all she got this guy to promise her when he thought she was a wealthy, moral-less businessman looking to buy a few young girls. Mr. Palmer began with the simple questions. "Please state your full name."

"Montana Jensen."

"And please tell the court what you do for a profession."

"I am a Special Agent for the FBI criminal division for Violent Crimes."

"What, exactly, does that mean?"

"Mostly, I work crimes against children."

Once the prosecution was satisfied, the defendant's young lawyer began his cross-examination. "Ms. Jensen, you stated you work crimes against children?"

"That is correct."

"And the prosecutor calls it human trafficking. Would you explain what that is?"

"Yes, sir. Human trafficking is the selling of a person for sex. Usually, the people who run it are the same people who traffic drugs and weapons. They come to realize that selling people is more profitable and less risky. People are a resalable commodity. Over and over again. In the case of a sex slave, that might be ten, twenty, or even as much as forty times a day."

As she talked, Tana was distracted by a young man who quietly entered the courtroom through the door in the back and slid behind the prosecution. Though she continued her dialog with the defense attorney, Tana was a bit unnerved by this man's constant eye contact. Every time she glanced in his direction, his eyes were intently watching her.

"Ms. Jensen?" The defense attorney's tone snapped her back to the situation at hand.

"Oh, I'm sorry. Would you repeat the question?"

"Would you explain your job to the court, please?"

"Yes, sir. It is my job to create profiles online, essentially posing as men looking to have sex with children. My goal is two-fold. First and foremost, we want to rescue these children. Second, we want to arrest those who profit from this behavior."

"Isn't that lying to people?"

"I object to answers to broad questions regarding the witness's integrity."

"Objection sustained," the judge answered.

"I'll reframe the question. Noble as that sounds, are you not just lying to anyone looking at that profile?"

"Call it whatever you like. If this problem is left unchecked, it will only continue to grow. The stats are overwhelming. Women and kids trapped by traffickers are forced to have sex with seven to ten thousand men a year. Roughly every thirty-nine minutes, a new porn video is created with some of these same children. Every single day sees new images of child porn uploaded to the web.

"The sex abuse of one child in front of a live webcam is estimated to generate revenues of thousands of dollars in one night, conservatively. To accomplish my goal, I have to become the very thing those men are looking to attract. And my goal, sir, is to put abusers of those little children and young women behind bars. Unlike your apparent goal of keeping them out."

The back door swung open, again breaking her concentration. A man entered and walked swiftly to the defense's side. His steely gray eyes could make a person's blood run cold if he were trying to intimidate them. Tana recognized the man instantly. Belmont Cooper. The big man in the law firm. This man always gave Tana a sick feeling, though she could not identify the reason. As her mind tried to label her response, she wondered what he could possibly gain from representing this lowlife?

The court broke for lunch as soon as Tana finished. The perfect time for her to slide out and retreat to her home.

"Tana!" The prosecutor, a wiry, balding man with bright blue eyes, an easy smile, and a much harder edge, caught her before she could make her escape. "Brilliant testimony! I think you sealed the coffin, so to speak."

"Thank you, sir."

"You know, there used to be a saying in DC, there's a lawyer for every three thousand people. These days, it's more like one for every three." He grinned as he looked in the direction of the young man who had been watching her so keenly. "And now there's one more. Let me introduce you to Tate Palmer. He's new to the firm. I guess it doesn't hurt that he's my nephew too. Heck, I practically raised the boy after his daddy died."

"Not sure she needed to know that already, Uncle Lee." With a big, cheesy grin spread across his face, Tate extended his hand to Tana. "We are heading to Rosey's. Join us for lunch?"

"I figured there was a relation; you have the same eyes. Thank you so much for the very kind offer. However, I have a lot going on that

I need to get back to." It wasn't entirely a lie. "Maybe next time. It's very nice to meet you, Tate." She couldn't avoid the intensity in his blue eyes. Tana was unsure she had ever felt anything like it before. "Congratulations on the new job. Please excuse me, gentlemen." It was all she could do to keep from running down the hall.

Georgia, 2007

The door to the house was almost as dark as her soul felt. No lights on inside meant no one was home. That was good. Tana could hardly stand the look in their eyes, let alone their questions and demands. She unlocked the door, walked in, and relocked it behind her. She walked down the hall and into her bedroom without turning on any lights or stopping in any other room.

On the bed lay an envelope. Tana picked it up and saw it was from the school they had visited two months ago. She didn't know if she was hopeful they would admit her or willing for it to be a denial. If they accepted her, Tana could run from this house and the pressure to explain things she didn't understand herself. If the letter were a denial, she could stay where she somehow knew her mom and dad did love her. So much turmoil swirled in her mind. She didn't want to tell them how she felt or what she was thinking . . . she wasn't sure she knew what to think or feel. Or what they expected.

Nor did she know what to do with this Jesus they kept bringing up in conversations. Love? Really? What is that? Protection? Where was that? Guidance? She couldn't even see it. Nope. None of it made any sense to her eighteen-year-old mind.

She turned the envelope over and pulled at the flap, which gave way quickly. The letter inside announced the school was pleased that she had applied, that her grades and test scores were favorable, and that they were excited to have her join them in the fall.

Well, she was going to college. That should make Mom and Dad happy.

Los Angeles, 2016

The call left Silvia with a half-smile on her face. Greg sounded happy and excited to be doing all he was. Still, for the third time this week, he was calling to ask her if she was okay with him working later than planned. If it weren't so close to summer break, she would have had an issue with the whole thing.

She turned her chair around, surprised to be face to face with Renee Daniels, the assistant to her boss, Chuck Blue. "Oh, geez, Renee; you scared the life out of me."

Standing her five-foot-nine frame to its fullest height, Renee inquired, "What was that?"

"What was what?"

"That smirk." Renee paused as if to get a better look at Silvia. "Everything okay?"

"What's not okay?" Both women turned to see their boss standing in the door frame.

"I wish I knew, Chuck," Silvia sighed, her eyes dropping to the papers scattered across the desk. "That's the third time Greg has called to ask if he could work late."

"And you aren't okay with that?"

Absently, Silvia shuffled pages around. "I mean, on one hand, he's just a boy and should be outside playing ball with his friends. On the other hand, he seems to enjoy his work."

"But?" Chuck pushed a little harder.

"Chuck, sugar, are you asking if we need to be concerned about Greg?"

His eyes snapped to his assistant. Every time she called him "sugar," he was thrown back to his Southern roots, and he was never sure if he liked the reminder, though he did find it endearing. "That is exactly what I'm asking."

"Oh, I don't know. Something just seems off. And yet, he is keeping up with his homework, and school is almost out for the summer." She looked up at the couple standing on the other side of her desk. "Maybe I just miss my boy."

"Maybe," Chuck tentatively agreed. Before he turned to make his way to his own office, he added, "If you figure out it's more than just missing him, let me know if I can help you in any way."

Feeling a little shell-shocked, Silvia turned to Renee. "What does that even mean?"

"I'm not sure." Renee tried to offer a reassuring smile, though it was disconcerting to her as well. "I am never sure what that man's thinking." She paused and added with a smirk, "Just remember to tell Chuck Blue what he can do for you."

Chapter 7

Washington, DC, 2018

"I've been thinking . . . we never really talk about your parents." Tate held his breath, gauging her reaction before he continued. "It sounds like they went out of their way to help you get back into a—for lack of a better word—normal life. Why is it you don't talk about them? Do you ever see them?"

After spending most of the day talking, Tana and Tate had walked to dinner, and on their way back to her apartment, stopped at a park where they sat on a swing in a little gazebo. Together they watched the setting sun, Tate with his arm around her shoulders, Tana with her head resting on his chest.

Tana took a deep breath. "You know . . . they tried hard. However, they kept trying to tell me how wonderful it was that Jesus brought me home to them. I never understood that. This belief in a God who would let something like that happen to me and their ability to give Him praise for my return. I mean, if you believed such a God exists, why wouldn't you be mad that He let that mess happen? I don't understand giving praise for my return and giving him a pass on my abduction."

"Let me see if I understand your dilemma." Tate searched for the correct words, not wanting to be insensitive to her heart. "It sounds like you feel you were not worthy of being protected from the nightmare, but rather only celebrated for surviving it."

"Something like that. You know, I remember so many Saturdays when my mom would be 'busy.' I didn't understand why she would be out, but never open about where she was going or what she was doing. Most of the time, she was rather chatty about her activities, even when I didn't ask questions. But these Saturdays, like maybe once a month, she said nothing. When I was seventeen, I overheard Mom talking with Uncle Troy. They were discussing a guy named Jack Beacher and how Mom was visiting him in prison." Tana turned and faced him. "Turns out, Jack is the man who put me in the van. He was the reason I couldn't sleep, the reason for my pain. And she was spending time talking to him. To say I felt betrayed anew is an understatement." She turned her head back to the west and snuggled into Tate's chest. "I left for college, and I never really looked back. I talk to them on the phone once in a while, but I bet it's been a couple of years since I've been home."

The silence was heavy until Tate spoke again, almost in a whisper. "I've gotta wonder if they weren't right about the protection." Tana jerked her head off his chest.

"What?" She blinked a couple of times, trying to determine his tone. "Seriously?"

"Think about this: What happened to you was horrible. No one should ever be treated the way you were. But there are those who cannot handle it as well as you did; they are not as strong as you. There are others out there who will not recover as well as you have. Still others, no matter how well you do your job, who will never be rescued. They have died, or will die, where they are. I know you see it every day . . ." He paused for a deep breath, knowing she might not like what he would say. "Maybe someone *was* watching over you."

She studied his face then gave him a glimpse of her past. "Praying for me, my mom would say." She absently touched her scar as she thought about her mom. "You know, when I first came back, I had nightmares all the time. I would wake up screaming, thinking I was back in that prison. I felt like someone was holding me down in the dark, and I couldn't breathe.

"Comfort was a fleeting mist, noticeable but uncontainable, and just out of my grasp. Mom would come into my room, and she would comfort me. Hold me, sing to me, whatever it took to settle me down. Mostly she would pray." She turned back to the sunset and settled once more into the warmth of his embrace. "I can't tell you how many mornings I woke up and she was still in my room. At first, she would kneel beside my bed—I think she spent the night like that. Later, once things had settled down some for me, she would sit in the chair in my room. I think she just fell asleep while praying for me."

"So . . ." Tate judged his words carefully, not wanting her to feel pressure or shame in what he was about to say. "What I'm hearing is the people who love you the most, lost you not once, but twice? I don't know how I would feel about the praying and whatnot, but it seems to me they did their best for you." Again he paused, but this time, he made sure to catch her eyes. "Do you think it's time to go back?"

As Tana let the idea bounce around in her head, she asked, "Have you ever considered the setting sun?"

"You mean the one we just watched?"

She giggled softly. "Not just that one, but in general—sunsets."

"Well, I guess the only thing I've ever considered about a sunset," he replied softly, "is how it would be a fabulous time to kiss a beautiful woman . . . if she was so inclined."

She turned to face him and feigned shock. "Why, Mr. Charming, are you trying to get fresh with me?"

He grinned at her. "Why, Ms. Jensen, I would never."

"Oh, that's too bad because I was kind of hoping you might."

Before Tana could finish her thought, Tate's mouth caught hers in a tender embrace. The initial surprise quickly gave way to her desire, and she found herself kissing a man back for the first time in her life.

The kiss slowed just enough for each to catch their breaths. "I will forever consider sunsets to be amazing," he breathed, without moving away from her. Their lips brushed together once more, gently and yet passionately.

She sighed deeply, "Um. Wow. That was a first."

"I have wanted to do that since I first saw you on the stand."

Tana laughed. "I am glad you waited. I would have punched you then."

Tate laughed with her. "I bet you would have. I'm thrilled you didn't this time."

"So I have a question for you now." She studied his face. "If you are serious about me seeing my parents, would you consider going to Georgia with me?"

He kissed her again. "I would be honored."

Georgia, 1998

Jack sat with cards in his hand, his back to the large television blaring music of some awards show no one seemed to pay attention to, the chatter in the room nearly overpowering the sound of voices and strings mingling. "This is getting ridiculous," he mumbled as he tossed his cards on the pile in the middle of the table. "I'll take two more."

"Man, you going to start that again? That's all you wanted last night."

"What? It's the first round of the night."

"Seriously, that's all you ever want." The large, dark eyes across from him sparkled with mischief. "Are you sure you know how to play this game?"

Jack glared across the table, irritated by the smirk on the man's face. "Angel, I . . ." he began but cut his thought short and whipped his head around to the screen behind him. He sat motionless for a few minutes.

Within my heart, my secret lies . . .

"What . . ." the man known to the group as Angel questioned Jack's behavior.

"Shhhh!" Jack commanded as he stood, quickly moving toward the television and turning up the volume. The room settled in hushed awe as the men watched the heavyset woman singing the high and low notes of an opera in front of a large orchestra, her range larger than most of their vocabulary.

"What's your deal, man?" questioned the man who had been on Jack's left, as his eyes looked from Jack's backside to the television and back. Mesmerized by the images before him, Jack ignored the inquiry. The man, known as Detox, turned to Angel. "Are we playing or what?"

Angel stood and moved beside Jack, where both were awestruck by the power of the vocals pouring from the small speaker. Lifting his voice just above a whisper, Angel wondered, "Who is that?"

Jack continued to ignore the questions as Detox joined them in front of the screen, taking note for the first time of the woman. Shocked by Angel's admission, Detox demanded, "Are you serious? Are you that uneducated in music? Man, that's Aretha Franklin."

"Shut up!" Jack snapped as a large choir backing the vocalist lifted their voices. "I'm trying to listen."

The two stopped their conversation as Aretha once more belted out the operatic lyrics.

Jack turned to the one man originally watching the show. In a hushed voice, he asked, "Why is she there?"

"It's the *Grammys*, man," he answered, confused by the question.

"Clearly, Einstein. But why is Aretha Franklin singing opera?"

"Oh. Sting said the guy scheduled, Pavo-something or other—"

"Pavarotti?"

A grin broke over Einstein's face. "Yeah, that's it. Sting said he was supposed to sing it, but his doctor said he was too sick, so they asked her to cover for him, 'cuz she sang it somewhere a couple of nights ago."

"So I'll ask again," Angel jumped back into the conversation. "Who is she?"

Detox turned back toward the abandoned card game in frustration, muttering, "I just told you, man."

The comment wiped the smile from Einstein's lips, and Jack winced. "How do you not know Aretha Franklin?" Einstein grilled him. "She's only the Queen of Soul."

"Soul? I don't listen to old people music," Angel retorted. "I'm more of a rock-n-roll guy."

"Rock-n-roll?" Jack repeated, the edge in his voice slicing the words. "Yeah."

"Ten years ago this woman was inducted into the Rock-n-Roll Hall of Fame," Jack answered, trying to not let his frustration show.

Einstein looked around Jack at Angel. "You ever see *The Blues Brothers*, man?"

Angel chuckled, "Yeah, that's a funny movie."

"Remember the waitress? The one signing?" His voice raised an octave as he sang the lyrics from the movie.

Detox jumped in right behind with his voice to add to the song, and the two guys croaked out the tune together.

Watching two of the toughest guys on the block singing in pitchy voices, Angel laughed as he answered, "Sure! She was all over that guy."

"Right. That was Aretha Franklin." He looked to Jack. "And to answer your question, she was there to do a Blues Brother's bit."

Jack didn't hear him. His eyes were focused on the woman on the television, but his mind was a long way off, fixed on another woman. Those legs. That hair. The words demanding respect tumbling from those lips.

Karaoke night at the campus bar, which meant the bar across the street from the campus. It was the first time he had set eyes on Leigh, and his heart was more her's with every beat of the drum and blast of the horn.

Los Angeles, 2016

Music pounded throughout the house. The thump of the bass was as inescapable as the thick haze of smoke hanging in the air, and people were everywhere. Tired and ready to go home, Greg found it all overwhelming. The adults. The other kids. The crazy nearly sexual games they all wanted to play. Some of it was funny and Greg found himself laughing. Some of it made him feel uncomfortable, and he found himself laughing to hide his unease.

For the third night in a row, Stan had told him to tell his mom he was working late but, instead, had taken him to a huge house party. The houses were full of people, some of them big names in the business, some of them government people Stan's Dad brought with him.

Tonight's party was no exception. From the moment they had arrived, it was a non-stop crowd. Greg smiled, talked to, and laughed with as many people as he could, but by 10:30, he knew he was ready to leave.

He moved toward the back door, looking for some fresh air, and spotted a basketball court. He looked back over his shoulder to gauge how much he would be missed. Determining that level to be low, he pushed the door open, stepped into the fresh air, and felt the immediate release of pressure on his eardrums. He made his way down the stairs to the pathway that lead to the pavement capped by two poles holding the backboards in the air. He scanned the area in the dark, hoping to find a ball. Disappointment replaced the hope as he found nothing.

"I wondered where you disappeared to."

Greg spun on his heels, his heart pounding in his chest. He saw Stan moving to the right of the stairs. A nervous chuckle slipped by his lips. "Hey, Stan. You scared me."

Stan opened a door Greg had missed under the patio and pulled out a ball. He tossed it between his hands a few times before he sent it in Greg's direction. "Looking for this?"

"Yeah. Thanks," Greg answered as the ball bounced in front of him and into his hands.

"Up for a game of HORSE?" Greg looked at the older man without answering. "You do know how to play HORSE, don't you?"

"Yeah," Greg answered before taking a deep breath. His shoulders dropped, though he kept his head held high. "I just haven't played since Dad . . ."

"Awe, man." Stan moved closer to the boy. "I'm so sorry, buddy."

"It's okay. I know you didn't know."

He knelt before the boy, making himself eye level with him. "We can do something else."

Greg shook his head. "No. I would like to play."

Stan smiled. "If you are sure. We could play in honor of your dad."

The idea made Greg smile. "Playing in Dad's honor; I'd like that."

Virginia, 2007

The campus was bright green, warm, and inviting, even if it was small. Small was probably better for Tana—fewer people to avoid. As she walked across the courtyard separating the cafeteria from the dorms, her eyes caught a glimpse of the setting sun. Bright colors screaming across the fading horizon stopped Tana mid-stride. The hues of pink and orange mingling with the darkening blue sky and a few cotton ball clouds captivated her, arresting her full attention.

"Gorgeous, isn't it?" Tana jerked her head to her left to find a woman standing next to her, an easy grin on her face. "I'm sorry, I didn't mean to startle you."

"I—I didn't hear you walk up."

"I don't think I've had the chance to meet you; I'm Dr. Kay Stoltenberg, the psychology professor."

"Tana Jensen, freshman."

"Nice to meet you, Tana Jensen, freshman, and obvious aficionado of amazing sunsets. Tell me, what do you see when you watch the sunset?"

Tana turned back to the sifting splashes of orange and pink and pretended to study them in their continued steady descent into bright purples and inky blues. Her mind raced with the sudden interruption and inquiry, frozen with the imposition of an explanation she didn't have.

"Yeah, they leave me pretty speechless too." The undaunted professor continued, undeterred by the lack of any form of acknowledgment. "I think it's because they help settle my soul, bringing life-giving peace. A type of grounding. That's their created value. It's not defined anywhere; it's just known. Even when we don't have the words to tell how we know, we just know."

Tana turned back, trying to figure out where this woman was headed and why she felt the need to drag Tana with her. Her eyes were again met with an easy, comforting grin. "I am of the opinion every freshman needs to learn this definition of value because knowing the value of something as simple as a sunset will help them discover their own deeper value." Tana could feel the blank stare cementing itself on her face. What did this woman mean by value? As if on cue, Dr. Stoltenberg added, "Knowing your value will help you excel in your studies and ultimately in life."

Tana turned her eyes to the diminishing sunset as the idea tumbled in her brain. She took a breath before she turned back to ask for clarification. But Dr. Kay Stoltenberg had left her side, and the courtyard, as fast as she had come.

Georgia, 2018

Praying. It was the only thing that kept Millie Jensen steady. And hymns. If not for the comfort and strength she found in the old songs, she would have little to hold onto. The words in the Bible could feel so far removed from all she had been through if not for the hymns that confirmed those words in her very bones. Millie half-watched the birds dance around the feeder outside her window while softly singing to herself.

Come thou fount of every blessing, Tune my heart to sing thy grace.
Streams of mercy never ceasing, Call for songs of loudest praise.

It was a distraction to her mind as much as the birds outside her window. With the loss of her daughter, bringing her back for the six years Tana lived with them, and the little contact they now had, she would be a brittle, bitter woman who would shatter with the slightest brush of a feather.

Teach me some melodious sonnet, Sung by flaming tongues above.
Praise the mount I'm fixed upon it, Mount of Thy redeeming love.

The prayers were a lifeline, and the hymns were grips for her tattered soul. She let the warmth of her tea slide down her throat, a balm for her weariness. The dance of the birds was interrupted by the metallic clanging of the phone sitting at the end of the couch. Such a love-hate relationship with that thing. "Good morning," Millie answered.

"Mom, if you have some time for me, I want to come home."

Was this a question?

"Montana Grace, I will always have time for you. When can you be here?"

Los Angeles, 2016

Stan's numerous silly antics on the court broke the heaviness in Greg's heart, and the laughter helped him relax more than he had in the last four or five days. Taking note of the change in the young boy, while standing under the basketball hoop, Stan told Greg, "It's great to see you smile. You have a wonderful smile."

"You're funny. That helps me smile," Greg added as he heaved the ball toward the backboard towering over him in the night sky. The ball slipped through the net with a swish.

Stan caught it mid-air. "No way. Lucky shot."

"Was not."

"Oh, yeah? Prove it," Stan demanded as he tossed the ball in Greg's direction.

The ball hit his fingers, and he shot it right back to Stan. "That's not how this game works. It's your shot." He pointed to his feet. "From right here."

"I'm not the shot you are," Stan complained as he moved toward Greg. "I never was very good at shooting free throws."

Greg watched the older man's awkward attempt at a shot. "Your form is horrible," he told Stan, a slight giggle in his voice.

"Oh, yeah? Where did you learn to shoot the ball?"

Greg lined up for another shot. "My dad taught me," he answered quietly as he let go of the ball again. This one hit the backboard flat and bounced back toward him.

Once more, Stan lined up to take a shot. "You and your dad were close, huh? What else did the two of you do together?"

Greg lined up for a shot from the left of the board, "Oh, you know, the usual stuff dads do with their kids." Stan didn't answer but waited for Greg to continue. "Swimming, biking, skateboarding, fishing. He came to my games. Taught me to play cards. Pretty much everything."

"Did he teach you about sex?"

"What?" Greg let out a nervous laugh.

"I'm just wondering if he had time to teach you all you need to know."

Greg focused on the backboard. "Uh. I guess we talked a little." He pushed the ball into the air but fell short of even catching the rim this time.

"Have you ever see a naked old man before?"

Facing Stan for the first time since the conversation became uncomfortable, Greg asked once more, "What?"

"Like did you ever see your dad get out of the shower? Or standing in the men's room?"

Greg shrugged. "I guess so. I never really thought about it."

"What about kids at school? You ever talk about sex with your friends?"

"You know I'm only ten, right?" Again, Greg shrugged. "I guess we mostly talk about school and basketball." He turned and scanned the dark edge of the court, looking for the ball. He spotted it just inside the tree line.

Stan followed the boy to the trees. Just as Greg reached the ball, Stan reached him. He grabbed his shoulders and turned the boy to face him. He pushed Greg back against the tree. His voice low, Stan growled, "Let me show you."

"What's going on here?" an unfamiliar voice boomed. Greg felt relief flood his body as Stan pulled back, though his hands didn't let loose enough for him to get away.

As quickly as the relief came, it left when Stan smiled at the man with the voice. "Come join the party, Dad."

Chapter 8

Washington, DC, 2017

Once she had the car on the freeway, Tana began to relax. Court days always made her so tense. Or maybe it was just the people. Tana was never sure which made her crazier, the number of bodies in a particular area or the traffic in town. Navigating the one-way streets going opposite directions or driving around a block can take three minutes or thirty, all depending on the time of day; judging the time one will be in the city was a crapshoot.

The crowds made her feel closed in, pinned down, and trapped. And it didn't take many bodies around her to feel like she was in the middle of Times Square. Even still, somewhere in her heart of hearts, she needed a connection, an anchor in the storms that raged inside her, a blanket for the scared little girl running wild in her mind. Goodness, she longed to trust more than she did. She yearned to trust someone enough to know them soul to soul, to be known deeply. Tana feared such authentic knowledge wasn't possible.

Startled from her thoughts by the shrill ringing of her phone, she glanced at a number she didn't recognize. She sent the call to voice-mail, then she reached over and turned up the music to drown the voices in her head.

A few moments later, Tana's phone rang again. Her least favorite thing about her music being stored on her phone was the interruptions, even the short blast of a text message impacted her listening. This time, she smiled when she glanced at the screen. Here was the one who knew her better than most and still cared enough to check-in. Cared enough to walk her through growth and pain and was still by her side whenever she needed her.

"Hi, Sunset Aficionado! Just a quick note to remind you how much value you bring to the lives you are touching. Keep being amazing in this lackluster world, my dear! Much love always." How did Kay always know when she could use encouragement?

Georgia, 2018

Jack paced the aisles of the library, not looking for anything specific. Rather, his mind raced through years of conversations with Millie. Intermingled with these conversations were emotions he never expected. How on earth did he come to this? What was it about this woman? How is it that she turns his world upside down?

If he were honest with himself, the "How on earth did he come to this?" question started a lifetime ago. Another time, another place, another mindset. The heart of the question beats with mistrust, gambling, uncertainty, and probably too much alcohol.

As he walked, he half-read the titles on the books. Maybe half-read isn't even correct. More like pretended to read. While turning his head to the right and back, something caught his eye. He stopped, turned back, and looked more closely.

The leather-bound book was pristine. Seemingly, very few hands had held this one. And yet, when he pulled the Bible from its perch, he could see some of the edges were frayed.

What was it Millie had quoted? Something about Romans. As he flipped the pages, he was unsure of what he was looking at. He didn't know how to even begin to understand how any of it was laid out on the page. Columns, rows, and added notes at the bottom made it hard to decipher the best place to begin. His mind raced. Millie wouldn't be back for another month.

"Hey man, you okay?" Jack spun around to find a short, light-skinned, dark-haired man with a thick beard standing behind him. His dark eyes twinkled with a warmth Jack didn't encounter often behind bars. In front of them, either. "Can I help you with something?"

"I don't know. Who are you?" Jack stumbled over his words.

Unfazed, the stranger returned a gentle answer. "Brother, my name is Daniel, and I'm a library volunteer. What can I help you with?"

Shoving the Bible at Daniel, Jack asked, "That depends. Do you know how to read one of these?"

Daniel grinned; his thick, black beard couldn't hide the round cheeks on either side of his smile. Something about this guy reminded Jack of a young Santa Claus, but darker. "Actually, yes I do. What are you looking for?"

"I had a lady tell me something about . . . um . . . Roman something or other."

"Romans. Great book. However, if you want to understand what Romans is telling you, you should start with the Gospel of John."

"What is that?"

"Come." Daniel pointed to a small table and chairs tucked in close to a wall with high windows that let a little sunlight into the dark room. "Let's sit down, and I'll show you."

Washington DC, 2018

Arriving home from work a little later than she wanted, Sonja felt hurried and frustrated. She dropped her bags on the kitchen counter and ran upstairs to her bedroom. Tossing her work clothes toward the hamper, she threw on a pair of jeans and some boots and grabbed a button-down shirt, which she buttoned as she walked back out of the room. "Hey, cowboy," she called to Tate as she hurried past his room. When she saw his suitcase lying on his bed, she stopped and turned. "Hey, cowboy, what's going on?"

"Hi! Come talk with me a bit, Nini?" Sonja eyed him carefully, then walked into the room, studying the contents he placed into the bag as she went. Toothbrush and toothpaste. Razor. Shorts and T-shirts. Dress slacks. "Do you like the green tie or this blue one with this shirt?"

Looking up, she answered, "Either works, but the blue one's my favorite." She watched him work meticulously for a few minutes before saying anything else. "What's going on?" His smile could melt her heart any time he needed it to. Oh, such a handsome young man, with his mother's smile. Sonja saw Carleigh every time something delighted him. She missed her best friend every time he smiled.

"I had the most fantastic discussion with Tana tonight." Sonja realized he was still talking to her.

She picked up a sock roll, "And so you're moving in?" she asked as she tossed it at him.

Catching it, he laughed. "No, silly." He dropped it back in the suitcase. "Hey, where's Uncle Lee? I wanted to talk to you both."

"Sounds serious. I don't know. I was kind of hoping you could tell me. I was running late for our Bible study and don't know if I should meet him there or here."

"I have not heard anything from him."

Just then, the sound of the garage door opening caught their attention.

"Good; he's home." She gestured toward the stuff on his bed. "Then you can explain yourself."

Georgia, 2018

The flight from DC to Atlanta runs about two hours. Tana wouldn't hear of Millie and Dave picking them up, so they had to wait the extra hour and a half before they could see her. Millie stood near the large picture window and watched a butterfly dance outside, vaguely aware of the gentle warmth of the coffee cup in her hands, as Dave walked into the room.

"You're up early. It's going to be a busy day, tomorrow even bigger. Are you rested enough?"

"It's not that early, dear." Millie turned from the window to face her husband. "This is my second cup of coffee already." Millie smiled at him.

"Only two? I've seen how you drink coffee when you are nervous; two can go fast. Tomorrow is a big day, so three or four easy."

"Yes, Dave, dear. It is a big day. I'm trying to pace myself, going over my list of things I must do today. I'm a little nervous, and very excited about seeing our baby girl. Has it been two years?'

"Mmmm, I think so. That's something I can't contemplate without my cup of coffee."

Millie laughed. "Let's fix that for you." She tucked her arm in his, and they walked toward the kitchen. "Incidentally, what do you think about Montana bringing home a boy? I'm not sure I ever really thought that would happen."

"It is a bit of a mystery," Dave agreed.

Pulling a cup down from the shelf, Millie continued, "I have been trying to come up with the conversations I have had with Tana over the last couple of years. I can't remember one, not even once that she ever said anything about anyone she worked with or spent any time with, let alone a boy."

"A boy she was interested in enough to bring home."

"Right? Tana doesn't even bring herself home, so this boy must really be something."

Dave studied his wife. The years ran together and had been so hard on them, but she still took his breath away. So beautiful. Despite it all, she remained tender to the Lord and gracious with him. "Honey, you have prayed for nothing less her entire life. How are you surprised that Jesus would bring a man into her life who could bring her home?"

She smiled at him again and handed him a full cup of steaming black coffee. "I don't know, Dave. I guess part of me gave up hope this would ever happen. All I know is we have to be especially kind to this boy. If he could bring our little girl home, he must be really special."

Washington, DC, 2018

"Upstairs, honey!" Sonja leaned over the balcony and called to Lee. "In Tate's room."

Placing his things on a small table by the garage door, Lee made his way up the back stairway and around the corner of the door. "Why are we hanging out here?"

"Because Tate has some news he wants to share." She smiled slyly at him. "With the both of us."

"Both of us?" Lee leaned down and kissed his wife. "Must be serious." He turned to Tate as he sat beside Sonja on the bed. "What's going on, boy?"

"You guys know I love you, right?"

"You are going to move in with her! I knew it!" Sonja jumped in the middle of his sentence.

"No one is moving in with anyone. I'm staying right here." He winked at Lee before adding, "For now." He quickly folded a shirt and dropped it into the bag. "I just want to make sure you guys know how much you mean to me. I mean, after Mom and Dad . . ." He hesitated a bit. Sonja wondered if there were tears in his eyes, but she didn't have a clear view of them. "Anyway, you guys are amazing, and I need to know that you know that."

"We love you, too, Tate." Lee pulled his wife closer to him.

He turned to face them. Sonja could see them sparkle, but they weren't teary. "Good. I want you both to be the first to know. Tana and I had an amazing conversation today, and we are flying to Georgia tomorrow afternoon to see her parents."

"Really? Why the rush?"

"Not a rush, but she hasn't seen them in over two years, and she needs to do so to work on her healing."

"Healing?" Sonja more repeated than questioned him.

"Yeah, healing. Her life has been beyond tragic, and when she is okay with it, I will fill you in. However, right now, I need to tell you I am in love with her, and I intend to ask her father for permission to marry her while we are there."

"What? Oh, Tate!" Sonja jumped up and threw her arms around the boy's neck. "I'm so excited for you."

"I don't know how soon she'll be ready, Uncle Lee," he said as he read the questions on his uncle's face. "So I don't know how soon the actual proposal will happen. I just want you to know it's coming."

Georgia, 2018

Daniel walked Jack through several verses, chapters, and books, hitting high points as he went. "See, if you start at the beginning of the whole book, also known as the Old Testament, we find a book called Genesis.

I won't go into the whole thing, but if you read it, you read a tale of love, loss, and seeking. For now, let's start in the New Testament and look at this, brother." He tossed most of the pages to the other hand and started flipping through others with the precision of an expert marksman. "There is a guy; he has two sons. One of them stops the father one day and says, 'Hey, I want my half of your property.'"

Jack's eyes grew wide. "Before he died?"

Daniel nodded. "Yep, while the father was still alive."

"He's a bold little snot!"

"Yes, he was. Even worse, when he got the money from his dad, he took off. Went to another country and blew it all."

"Everything?"

"Everything. He had parties with his friends; he lived it up until all the money he had was gone. And when he spent it all, the economy took a turn for the worse. Suddenly, there was no money, no food, and no friends. The boy got himself a job for a local farmer, who sent him into the fields to feed his pigs. Suddenly, this rich boy found himself slopping hogs! Have you ever slopped hogs, Jack?"

"Nope. I've spent time with people I would consider pigs, but no, not actual pigs."

Daniel smiled broadly. "Basically, pigs eat what humans don't. Leftover food and things like cucumber peels, apple cores, melon rinds, and stale bread. What's more, this kid was so hungry he wanted to eat what he was feeding those pigs."

Jack was enthralled and moved by Daniel's tenderness. He abruptly stopped the train of thought Daniel was following. "Daniel, let me ask you something? Why are you here? Right now?"

"Man, I'm here to talk to you."

"But you didn't know me before you saw me standing there. You don't know me now. So, why? Why did you walk into this prison this morning? I mean, you are a guy who doesn't have to be behind these bars, and yet you choose to be. I mean, you opt to be here!"

Daniel chuckled softly. "Jack, do you know anything about me? What I do for a living? My history? My family?"

"Dude. I've never even seen your face before today."

"I spend most of my days leading a modest company. I have about five hundred employees. We make money and keep our customers happy. I have an amazing wife and four adorable kids. I get to go where I want and do as I see fit. I spend time with my friends and extended family. Yes, I guess as you see it, I have a choice. But I don't really. I have been adopted, changed, and given a new chance at the life I now lead.

"Life was not always this easy for me. I grew up in a rough area of Atlanta. I was rescued from the path I was on. My debt was paid, and I was taken into a family who loved me unconditionally. To honor the One who has given me such grace and honor, I choose, as you say, to lay down my life and give it back to Him by coming here. My life is an offering; my time is best spent serving those who know the honor they have been offered."

"So some rich family adopted you. It ain't that easy for most of us."

"No. Not a family. Well, kind of a family, but not like you think." Before Daniel could finish, the bell rang, indicating to the guys their time was up. "Shoot. I thought we had more time. Do me a favor. Start reading this in the book of John. Write down any questions you have. I'll be here next Saturday, and we can talk more then."

Los Angeles, 2016

Silvia Blakely turned the page back one and started to reread the paragraph. She was having trouble concentrating on the words, and she kept losing her place. It was nearly midnight—much too late for a young boy to be out. Even though she knew he was with Stan, she still found her world a little off-kilter when her boy wasn't home. "Oh, for heaven's sake," she spouted out loud as she tossed the book to her bedside. As if on cue, the sound of a slightly muffled engine stirred near her driveway, quickly followed by the thud of a door falling into place. "Finally," she murmured as she brushed the covers back and moved to greet her son at the front door.

She was nearly too late.

By the time she made it to the top of the staircase, Greg had descended the three stairs, the front door already shut and locked behind him. "How did it go, honey?" she called to him.

"Fine," Greg's body froze on the stairs, and he answered without looking back at her.

Something about his tone made her pause. "You okay, Greg?"

"Just tired, Mom," he sighed. "I just want to go to sleep."

"Oh. Okay." Silvia felt a bit lost. Greg's late nights over these last months had begun to create a crater in her heart. "Well, if you're sure you are alright . . ."

"I'm fine, Mom," he snapped more harshly than he intended. "I just want to go to bed."

"Well," she still hesitated. "Okay. Good night, then."

"Good night," he called as his feet hit the bottom of the stairs, and he disappeared into the dark hallway.

Chapter 9

Georgia, 2006

"Virginia? Are you sure South University is where you want to go?" Millie could feel the distance between them growing already. She wanted to reach out, pull Montana close, and never let go. However, in her heart, she knew that would only stifle her baby girl.

"Yes, Momma. I need to help make sure what I went through doesn't happen to other little girls, and a Criminal Justice degree seems to be the best way."

"Baby, you know you alone can't stop evil in this world."

Tana didn't hesitate. "No, but there are thousands sold into trafficking each year; if I can help save some of the girls, maybe I can slow it down."

Millie studied her daughter, thinking to herself, *One has to admire the strength in this little powerhouse—maybe little isn't the best word; she's a beautiful woman now, Millie! All she endured, and she wants to fight for other little girls. That scar on her face, now faded and healed, but still visible, is a constant reminder of her missing years.* She let her eyes meet Tana's, "Okay, baby. We will support your decision and continue to pray for you."

Washington DC, 2018

Tana was beginning to question if the flight to Atlanta and upcoming drive from the airport to Greensboro was long enough. The butterflies in her stomach were much too active. Even Tate wasn't much comfort right now. How did she let him talk her into this?

Looking out the window, it always amazed Tana how things seemed to slow down once the plane was in the air. Nothing but clouds below them and the setting sun to watch. She found herself mesmerized by the bright orange and pink hues swirling together as the sun sank below the cotton ball clouds. She began to think about Professor Stoltenberg and her ability to just waltz into her space when Tana needed her most—what Kay would say and how she probably wanted the interruption the least. Tana remembered she had been sitting in a campus coffee shop when Kay had walked in. What was that, her junior year? Yeah, her junior year. She hadn't been in Kay's class for a couple of years and had only seen her in passing when she walked into the coffee shop that evening.

"Well, hello, oh, Sunset Aficionado . . ." Tana chuckled a little at the familiar nickname.

"Good evening."

"Can I join you?"

Tana pulled her feet from the chair in front of her and sat a little straighter. "Of course. I'm not getting anywhere anyway."

"What's troubling you tonight?"

"Oh, you know, life."

"That's a big topic."

Tana chuckled again. "I suppose it is."

"Any particular area?"

"Right now, I'm supposed to be writing a paper on the characteristics of a pedophile. I'm trying to find value in the kids who have come out of such a situation. They all seem so damaged and broken."

"Maybe the issue lies within your question. The kids are not more or less valuable because of their abuse. Nor are kids more or less valuable when there is no abuse. They are valuable because they are children. Human beings. Real live people." Tana tried to blink away her confusion. Clearly, Kay read it all over Tana's face.

"Remember the sunset? This one tonight is not less valuable because it's less colorful than the first one we discussed. It's just different. When one observes many sunsets, even the lack of brilliant color has a beauty in its simplicity. When you study them, enjoy the beauty they offer, you are honoring that sunset, be it bold and beautiful or simple and sweet. Honoring the One who created it."

Kay paused, looking out the window and searching for her next words. She turned to Tana, who was still studying the hues before them. "You know, I think the more broken a person is, the more color they have. Like the sky after an intense storm is clear, bright, and colorful. You are a beautiful young lady, but your eyes tell me a deep, dark history is under close guard." Tana could feel her cheeks flush. "Your value isn't more than mine, but neither is it less than mine. I just think there is a deeper color than what you have shown before."

"Are you okay?" Tate's voice broke through her thoughts.

"Um . . ." Tana stretched as much as one can when stuck in a middle airplane seat. "My nerves are on fire, but other than that, I'm great." He smiled at her attempt to keep things light. Offhandedly, Tana added, "I'm pretty sure I would be more comfortable having a root canal."

Georgia, 2018

The conversation was shallow but comfortable at first. Introductions, of course—he should call them Dave and Millie or even Mom and

Dad, just not Mr. and Mrs. Jensen; he was to be comfortable and familiar. The weather, their trip, the rolling green hills of Georgia, the stories of the kids' first few encounters, and even their first dates were topics of conversation as they waited for the tea to brew on the stove. But Tana had an agenda, and Millie could feel it. As the four chatted, she also conversed with her Savior about her craving His wisdom, insight, and strength to guide her little girl. Rooms and rest, followed by breakfast the next morning.

Watching the ease of movement between Tana and Tate brought Millie a comfort she had not felt in years. Tate's ability to be so gentle and considerate with Tana both impressed and touched Millie. There was something about their relationship that had opened a door into Tana, and through it, Millie could see glimpses of her carefree four-year-old dancing for joy.

"What do you drive, young man?" Her husband asked Tate. God bless that man! Millie knew where Dave was steering the conversation. He could still make her heart skip a beat, even after thirty-three years.

"Currently, I drive a black 1999 Thirtieth Anniversary Ram Air Trans Am." Dave hit a nerve with this one, praise Jesus. Millie could see it coming. The twinkle in Tate's eye matched Dave's. Car junkies.

"That's a nice ride. Nice ride. But I can do you better."

A lazy smile slid on Tate's face, "Oh, yeah? How's that?"

"Oh, no, you didn't just ask . . ." Montana laughed, and Millie's heart jumped inside her. That laugh was music to her ears. "You are about to get the full load, Tate Palmer."

"Wanna see my ride?" Dave asked the boy. "A Tuxedo Black 1969 T-Top Stingray, 427 under the hood."

"No, you don't," Tate laughed. "Seriously?"

"Yes!"

Washington, DC, 2017

That voicemail. Tana was not sure what to do about the voicemail. She turned them down for lunch today, so this Tate guy—the same one who kept staring at her—he was the one who called while she was driving home, the unknown number. Something about wishing his uncle had a reason for him to call, and he had to try to make something up when all he really wanted was to take her to dinner.

Tana had to listen to the message four times to convince herself he was serious. Who was this guy? He didn't ask her to call him back. Said he would call her back. Ugh. Tana wondered how many times she would have to ignore a call from him before he understood the answer was no, though she did have to admire his tenacious persistence.

Georgia, 2018

Something about being home eased Montana more than she expected. As she watched Tate with her parents, the years and angst she had harbored in her heart seemed to melt like butter on a hot pan. So much so, Tana was surprised by her voice as the question tumbled from her lips. Maybe the ease she felt actually made asking easier.

Millie was not blindsided by Montana's question, and still, the hit sucked even more life from her body.

"I need to understand why you betrayed me, Mom."

Without any further explanation, Millie knew to what her daughter referred. Oh, how she needed the right words here. Now. Jesus, please. "Baby doll, I never betrayed you. You always have been and always will be my very life. Everything I do is to help you grow and become who you are meant to be."

"How is that even possible?" Tana could feel frustration cresting at the edge of her eyes, trying to burn its way out of her tear ducts. "You spent so many Saturdays going to talk to that man. My abductor." She paused, trying to control the fire of anger that threatened to consume her. Tana took a deep breath, willing the quiver in her voice to settle, "The very reason I couldn't sleep was taking my mother from me."

"Baby, he was giving you back your mother . . ." Millie hesitated, trying to slow the tidal wave of emotions drowning her. "Visiting Jack was the hardest thing Jesus asked me to do. It was harder than living eight years not knowing if my baby was even alive. Facing the very reason my heart shattered was like facing the devil himself. But I wanted desperately to be strong for you, to be whole for you, if God brought you back home. And I needed to be whole for myself and your dad if He did not. The more I read the Bible; the more Jesus made it clear to me, I could never be either if I didn't forgive Jack."

The tears escaped Millie's eyes, and she looked down at the teacup in her hand. "I started reading the first chapter of Colossians, where Paul talks about Jesus rescuing me from my darkness by forgiving my sins. I knew the only way I could be whole was to begin to offer the same forgiveness I received." She paused and took a deep breath, her fingers tracing the edge of the cup.

"It took years of looking him in the eyes and saying the words before I meant them. My broken heart was such a stone, just saying it once was worthless. I was like a child throwing a tantrum, and Jesus had to slow me down and make me repeat it over and over." She looked up from her teacup into the face of her beautiful daughter. "Four years. I needed four years of monthly visits before my heart cracked open, and I meant it. And it was after that Jesus allowed you to come home to me."

"Wait. What? I thought you started visiting him *after* I was home."

"No, baby. Paul came to me with news they had a lead in your case on your eighth birthday." Memories of that day flooded her mind, "I was feeling so sorry for myself at the time." Millie could feel shame rolling in like a storm cloud covering the sun, threatening a downpour. Her eyes fell to her teacup, her finger tracing slow circles around the lip.

Montana watched her mom's finger and wondered if she would rub the gold trim off the cup. "I am not proud of my whining to Jesus about how unfair life was. That I could not celebrate with my baby girl, my only child, my flesh and blood, on her birthday. I was knee-deep in a pity party when Paul knocked on the door." She continued to breathe deeply and steadily.

"When Paul began to tell me the story, I knew. I could almost hear Jesus whisper in my ear about my love affair with legalism and my lack of real love. It wasn't a harsh conversation, like a scolding. It was gentle, tender, like the kiss of a mother on a child's scraped knee. Jesus asked if I wanted my little girl home and healed, and told me I had to know what it looked like to really love.

"Losing you crippled me. It took four years to begin to limp through life again. I began to realize that no matter what I lost, I still had God. I still had His forgiveness. That in every loss and every change I walked through, I kept God and God kept me. And in that knowledge, I realized that Jack did not have that same anchor for his soul to hold onto.

"Jesus wanted me to be able to dance. Even with that limp. I needed to learn to dance like a tree dances in the wind. As the branches are lifted and leaves are rustled by the wind moving through them, the roots dig deeper, hold stronger. I couldn't do that submerged in self-pity. It was like there was too much water in the ground, making it impossible to grab hold of anything. And as I leaned into what Jesus was asking, I began to see Jack in a different light. I began to understand he couldn't even move beyond the torment in his life if someone did not throw him a lifeline."

Millie looked back up from her cup and watched her daughter stare blankly out the window at the same bird dance she had watched a few hours earlier. Her heart flooded with a love she could hardly contain. This child, her little girl, this woman sitting before her, was breathtaking. Millie could only assume this was a small taste of God's love for Tana. She took a deep breath, "Montana Grace. Did I ever tell you why we chose this name for you?"

The question startled Tana. She turned her eyes to focus on her mom. Had she ever really looked at her before? Really? Her ice-blue eyes. That fine, white hair. The laugh lines on her freckled face. Even in her late sixties, her mother was stunning. The life that radiated from her was beyond her looks. There was something Tana could not quite put her finger on. "No. I don't think so. I guess I assumed it was from the state. I vaguely remember someone was from there—your mom, maybe?"

Millie giggled softly. "Actually, it was a friend's family I visited once or twice. Then I met your daddy. He loved the idea of the area, the wild west, so we visited a time or two before you came along."

The images flooded her memory of their younger selves, a much younger Dave and Millie, making her smile, and she lingered in the warmth they brought. "Montana means mountain. Grace is charm or favor." Millie let the words hang in the air, then turned her head to catch Tana's gaze. "From the moment I knew you were coming, I loved you with a wide-open love.

"However, when that nurse placed you in my arms for the first time, I thought my heart was going to burst from the mountains of love that exploded through it. I knew God was giving me a favor beyond any measure. Every name your dad and I had ever talked about was suddenly small and not fit for a child as beautiful as you. When I looked at him, I could tell he was feeling everything I was. 'God's grace is going to drown me. The sky of Montana ain't got nothing on this beauty' was all he could say." She smiled at the memory. "He's got a way with words, your dad. But I knew from that moment what your name would be."

Los Angeles, 2016

The morning light did not make anything better. As soon as his eyes opened, Greg felt his body flood with the nausea from the night before. His mind raced with questions and conversations as he dressed for the day, and even as his mom drove him to her office. Could he have done something to suggest an interest? Sitting at the break table, he could think of nothing.

"Hey, buddy, I didn't know you were here today." Greg looked up from the table to see his mom's boss standing in the doorway of their office breakroom.

"Hi, Mr. Chuck."

"Will you be here all day? I could probably find some cameras that need their batteries changed or set you up with a background to play with shots on."

Greg smiled slightly, "That's very kind, sir, but I am only here until Mom can get me to the studio." He looked up at the clock hanging above the door. "I'm supposed to be there at noon for makeup and hair."

"Noon? I'd better go find her, or you'll be late."

"Thanks," Greg mumbled as he hung his head again.

There was something about the boy's tone that stopped Chuck. He studied the boy for a moment. If his blond hair was straight, Chuck thought it might touch the top of the table. "Are you okay, son?"

Georgia, 2018

Dave studied Tate as he slowly moved around the car. By the questions the young man asked, Dave could tell he knew a good deal about cars. He found himself impressed by his knowledge. "You seem to know your way around an engine pretty well, young man. How does a lawyer find time to learn about cars?"

Tate laughed lightly. "I grew up tinkering with them. My Uncle Lee, it's his practice I now work for, he rebuilds cars as a stress reliever, and I was always underfoot, so he figured it was better to show me what to do rather than have me breaking things trying to learn about them."

"That's a good uncle."

"Yes, sir. He raised me well."

"Raised you?"

"Yes, sir. My parents, John and Carleigh Palmer, were killed in an accident when I was just a couple of years old. Uncle Lee is my dad's twin, and they were pretty close as kids, so I understand. He and Aunt Sonja took me in and raised me."

"Wow. I had no idea. Sounds like they are pretty amazing people."

"Yes, sir. The best." Tate had nearly crawled under the car.

"You know, Tana's not told us much about you."

Standing up and dusting himself off, Tate smiled at Dave. "No, sir, I suspect not. She has made it pretty clear she doesn't confide in many people, and that even talking with you guys has been hard." Tate grabbed a towel from the workbench and wiped his hands to settle the emotion swelling inside his chest. "I cannot imagine the hurt you and your wife have been through."

"It's not been an easy journey, for sure." He paused, studying this young man in front of him. *Be careful with him,* Millie had said. "That being said, it does not make me love my little girl any less, and that leaves me torn just a bit emotionally."

"Torn? How so?"

"Well . . ." Tate thought maybe there was a hint of mischief in the older man's eyes. "I'm trying to decide if I should be grateful you brought my little girl home or try to run you off for dating her."

Tate grinned at him. "I hope, sir, you'll choose the first and give me a chance before you try the latter. Can I make you a promise?" Tate didn't pause long; he didn't want to give Dave a chance to answer. "I will not be easy to run off. Tana tried. Hard. It took me a good six months to get her to go out with me the first time." Dave laughed out loud. "I wish I was kidding; she was tough on me! I had to get a case involving a child before she even agreed to coffee."

"Sounds like her mother in her. I told her I would marry her the first night we met. Millie told me I'd be lucky to get a first date."

Washington, DC, 2017

The buzzing of his phone would not stop. Tate could hear it as soon as he turned off the shower. He grabbed his towel and began to dry off, expecting the vibration to stop. As soon as it did, it began a second time. And a third. By the time he had his jeans on, it was on the fifth start.

Tate moved into his room and stopped at the dresser as he fastened the button on his pants.

"Good grief, don't you ever answer your phone?" Chuck Blue asked from the other line.

"I just did."

Across the country, Chuck scowled at no one in particular. "I don't have time for your cockiness today, buddy."

"Whoa, I haven't heard you this uptight since Mr. Gleaves failed your humanities paper in ninth grade. What's going on?"

"I have a lady working for me. Her son has started working in Hollywood."

Tate laughed again as he sat on the edge of his bed, pulling his shoes over and sliding his feet in. "I am not that kind of lawyer."

"Can I finish? This is in your neighborhood."

"Chuck, LA is nowhere close to my jurisdiction."

"I'm not talking about just LA. I'm talking DC. I'm talking about senators and other politicians involved. I'm talking about drugs, sex trafficking, and murder."

"You're not making any sense."

"I'm telling you, man, this kid needs protection, or he's going to end up dead. You need to find someone to guarantee his safety."

"Slow down, Chuck. I didn't say I couldn't make it happen. It just may take a bit." Tate chewed his lower lip in thought before he spoke again. "Start at the beginning and tell me what's going on."

Chapter 10

Georgia, 2018

Outside in the warm air, Tana felt some comfort—maybe it was just breathing fresh air. Thoughts tumbled inside her head like clothes in a dryer. She could feel the warmth of the spring evening, but also the cool darkness creeping from inside her soul. Thoughts of her abduction, her abductor, and her mother twisted her mind like a pretzel. She had hoped the clear air would help her make sense of it all, but the new information and old feelings swirled around like oil and water.

After their conversation about the car, Tate and her dad decided they would spend the following day fishing and were working out details for that trip. Her mom ran to the grocery for something before dinner. Wanting to erase the fog from her head, Tana felt the need to go for a run and was grateful everyone else had found something to do that didn't involve her.

The chirping from her phone would have been annoying, except it was one of a few numbers for which she set a custom tone. She knew without looking who was calling, and her heart almost jumped from her chest. She slowed her movement to answer the call.

"Hi! I've been thinking about you all day, and I just felt like I should check in on you. Are you okay?"

Tana almost laughed. "I don't know how you know just when to call. No, I'm not okay."

The professor took a deep breath. "I didn't think so. Are you ready to talk about it?"

"Here's the reality, Kay; I've been in a black hole almost my whole life. Like I fell into a deep well and cannot get myself out. I am desperate to get out, but I don't know where to turn."

Los Angeles, 2016

Stan West scanned the cafeteria for blond curls. He had not been able to pick Greg up that morning, so the boy's mom brought him in. He needed to see how Greg was doing after their late night. His eyes locked onto the head full of curls sitting at a table with Wade Bale and Georgia Collins. Looking at the back of the boy's head, he couldn't tell what his state of mind was. The faces of the two A-list actors appeared to show concern. The thought made him hesitate in the doorway.

Wade saw him and waved him over. "Hey, Stan! Greg was just telling us about last night." Stan's eyes shot toward Greg, and he felt his face flush. The boy turned his head toward Stan, a weak smile on his face, but his eyes would not meet Stan's. Bale continued as if he didn't notice the exchange between them. "He was telling us your dad is a senator. How did I not know this?"

Stan turned to the actor and forced a smile, "Did you not? I guess I didn't know that you didn't know." He giggled to himself and added, "When you are the child of a senator, you just think everyone knows your parents. I mean, you can't go anywhere with him that people don't know him."

Knowing his own struggle with fame, Wade laughed. "Yeah, I bet. It probably gets you into great restaurants though."

"Oh, man. The food I've eaten!" Once more, Stan shifted his attention to Greg. "Hey, I came to find you because I have great news." He didn't wait for a reaction from the boy. "Dad has more people he wants to introduce you to and since the film promotion is about to start, we are going to kill two birds with one stone, so to speak." As Stan's grin widened, Greg found himself surprised it could grow any more. In his excitement, Stan nearly stumbled over his words. "The studio is going to fly you to Washington DC in two weeks to do interviews and attend a couple of major political events while you are there. One of those events will be a party at the White House for school-age children to learn more about our political system. And you," Stan reached out and ruffled Stan's hair, "you get to be the guest of honor."

"Hey," Greg objected. "You're gonna get me into big trouble with Rosie!"

"Oh, right," Stan laughed. "I forgot you still have a scene to shoot. Isn't that exciting?"

"Yeah, I guess." Greg turned to Wade. "I need to get back to the set and run lines before we have to shoot. See you there."

Wade looked from Greg to Stan and back. "Hold up there, young man." Greg stopped and turned to face the two men. "I'll go with you." He nodded toward Stan. "But you have to remember how hard this guy is working for you. It takes a lot to get your name out there. To have major parties set up as soon as shooting is done? Well, that only helps us all. Make sure you are grateful for the work when people work for you."

Greg nodded and turned to Stan. "Thank you for your help, Mr. Stan. I appreciate you and your dad working that out for me."

Again, Wade corrected, "Us. By helping you, he's helping all of us."

"Yes, sir, Mr. Wade. Thank you for helping all of us." Then, he turned and ran down the hall.

Wade turned to Stan and shrugged his shoulders. "Kids. Am I right?"

Georgia, 2018

Jack paced the library floor like a caged animal—head down and chewing on his fingernails. Daniel spotted him through the glass in the door before he walked in. Just based on body language, he could not tell if Jack was excited or agitated.

Daniel pushed open the door. "Jack." His head jerked up, eyes wide and, maybe, Daniel thought, tired? Or maybe just wired. "How are you today?"

Moving toward Daniel quickly, Jack failed to answer the question. "He ran to him!"

"I'm sorry . . . What? Who ran?" Daniel moved behind the circulation desk and set his belongings down. He ushered Jack to sit at a nearby table, grabbed his coffee cup, and followed Jack to a seat. All the while, Jack seemingly rambled.

"The Father! The boy . . . with the pig slop . . . he went home . . . the Father! He ran! He didn't just meet him; he ran to him!"

Daniel chuckled at Jack's reaction as he pulled up his chair. "I guess you read some in the book, huh?"

Jack pondered the question and slowed his pace. "Well. Yes." Like a freight train gaining speed, Jack's thoughts busted from his mouth: "But mostly I read and reread this story. I can't figure this father out. I mean, his kid is an idiot. A spoiled brat. But the father took off running to greet him as soon as he saw the boy."

"Yes."

"And the other brother—dude was so mad at him, didn't even want to talk to him."

"Yes." Daniel grinned at Jack's enthusiasm.

"And the father went to him too."

"Yes."

"What kind of a man does that?"

This question caught Daniel off-guard. He looked up at Jack; something about the man had changed, and Daniel couldn't put his finger on it. Was that hope he saw in those eyes? He wanted more explanation, so he asked, "What do you mean?"

Softer, Jack slid into the seat across from Daniel, trying to bridge the chasm he faced between what he knew from experience and the information he had read. "What kind of a man seeks out someone who has wronged him—and not in a manner by which to get some revenge— but to build that other person up? I mean, he had been wronged by his son, and still, he threw him a party and celebrated his return."

"Well, a man who loves, honors, and respects the people around him. That father had a true love for his boy. Yes, he hurt, no doubt. But he missed his boy, which is an even bigger hurt. When he saw his son walking toward him, he didn't care that he had been wronged. He was just glad to see his son again. He was showing him the same love God has for us."

"And his older son?"

"The older boy was struggling with resentment, something I'm guessing you have also felt."

"Do people love like that? I mean, really? I've never . . ." Jack paused. Daniel could see him swallow hard.

"What?" Daniel leaned toward the man, speaking softly, bridging the gap the table created between them. "What did you just recall?"

"I think I know one who loves like that. The only person who ever treated me with any respect, before I met you."

"Who was that, Jack?"

"One of the people I hurt the most. Millie Jensen is probably the only person who has ever treated me with any respect in my whole life. I mean, I've had people who seemed to like me, only for them to take off when things got tough. But who has gone out of their way to be kind to me? Millie was the first—probably the only one. And honestly, I've treated her with little more than contempt."

As if he were waking from a long sleep, an idea began to form in Jack's mind, and he knew what he should do. What he had to do. It was time to come clean. He had known for a while, but he had never had the strength to take that step. He had spent nineteen years paying for this. It was time to stop protecting the guilty party. Not that he wasn't guilty, but others needed to pay for the part they played, and he was done protecting them. Jack no longer had anything to lose.

"Daniel, can you get me a meeting with the sheriff?"

Georgia, 2018

As they talked about all Tana had been through, Tana walked and Kay prayed. She needed the wisdom to help this girl. Tana's walk opened to the edge of the little lake bordering her parents' acreage. Here, she slowed her walk and paced the shoreline between a couple of trees.

"And so, I find myself at my parents' house because Tate figured it was time to bridge that gap. As I sat at their table, I found myself angry with the decisions that they've made. And angry about things I had no control over." Tana sighed deeply, running her free hand through her hair and back down along her jawline, the scar once again under her fingertips.

"The reality is my parents didn't have any control over much of it either. Even as I wrestle with the fact that I am angry with them, I am so very aware of how much of it was out of their hands. Like they wanted this to happen? That's the most ridiculous thing ever."

"Wow . . . slow down just a bit. That's a whole lot going on there. And not any of it is unjustified. So take it easy on yourself. Okay?"

"Okay. But I don't even know what that looks like."

Kay suppressed a laugh. "And that's okay. Repeat after me. That's okay . . ."

"What's okay?"

"Your emotions are okay—all of them are. It's normal to have all the feelings you're having. And to be wrestling with having them."

"Then why doesn't it feel okay?" Tana fought the brimming in her eyes.

"Because we live in a world with little honor and a big fear of vulnerability, where any remaining honor has been stripped away so nothing ever feels right. Everything is upside down and backward."

"I don't understand."

"Remember how we talked about the sunsets?"

"Of course."

Kay took a breath. "Each one, in its splendor and glory, was created with honor. And each time we see one, we are reminded, somewhere in our spirits, that there is a God who loves us. But there is also one who could not stand the honor God gave to the people He created and sought to destroy the relationship people had with God. So he nudged people to disobey God, and in that one act, he removed honor and brought in shame. And for someone like you, who has been dishonored so severely for so long, the concept of any honor being given or shown to you is unimaginable."

"I'm not sure I even understand the concept."

"That's exactly what I mean. When you look at yourself, you see this thing that happened to you, and it defines who you are in your mind. It's a scar that demands your attention, and you assume that is how everyone sees you. However, that's just not true. No one else looks at you and sees the monstrous scar you see. If anything, people look at you and see the beauty you have become. Because of all you have been through, you naturally lack the belief that you are worthy of that view, worthy of the honor. And because you lack that belief, you will have a hard time thinking about or accepting someone else honoring you. Remember how we talked about taking that leap of faith?"

"Sure."

"How did that work out?"

"Good. Tate has been fantastic."

"You have learned to love Tate more because of how well he has loved you. You have learned to step back and see and understand your parents a little more because of how well Tate has loved you. I think it's time to take another leap. To learn another new mercy. There is both vulnerability and strength in mercy."

"How so?"

"Remember, we learn mercy by experiencing mercy. The biggest show of mercy was God's mercy on us. We also learn to love when we experience love. The Bible tells us we love each other because He first loved us."

"And what is this mercy I need to learn?"

"The mercy of forgiveness."

Kay's words echoing in her ears made it tough for Tana to sleep. The house was still, and the moonlight poured in through her childhood window. She vacillated between feeling like the little girl she once was, who had just come back from her long nightmare, and the adult she now was. Tana wasn't sure how long she had been awake or if she had even gone to sleep. After knowing she was awake for a good thirty minutes, she decided maybe a cup of tea would help ease her thoughts and allow sleep to fill her eyes.

As she tossed back the covers, she reached over and grabbed her sweatshirt; the house was a bit chilly at nighttime. Without turning on a light, she found her sweatpants in her suitcase and pulled them on.

Tana headed toward the stairs and moved as quietly through the old house as her bare feet and the creaky floorboards allowed. As she turned the corner at the bottom of the stairs, she noticed the soft glow under the door to the kitchen. It was early, even by her mom's standards, to be up. She pushed the door softly, and it gave way to her touch, revealing it was not her mom who was up, but rather her dad. She smiled at the sight of him sitting at the head of the table, reading glasses perched on his nose, Bible laid flat on the table, cup cooling untouched.

Dave looked up from the book in front of him. "Hey, baby doll. What are you doing up?"

"I couldn't sleep—and I could ask you the same question," Tana responded, walking into the room and toward the table.

He smiled at her. "And I would give you the same answer. Sleep is an elusive beast tonight." She leaned down and kissed the top of his balding head.

"Yes, yes it is."

"Tea? The water on the stove is hot."

"Thank you." She moved back to the cabinets and pulled a mug down. "What are you drinking?"

"Chamomile. Thought it might help me sleep."

Tana laughed lightly. "How's that working out for you?"

Dave smiled at his daughter. "Well, nothing yet." He watched as Tana moved gracefully around the kitchen. It was almost as if she had never left. Or maybe just that they had not changed where anything was in the time she had been away. Either way, she had not forgotten where things belonged and had no trouble finding the tea. The thought of Tana being comfortable in their house made him smile.

Tana turned, warm mug in hand, in time to see her father's delighted grin. It made her chuckle. "What are you grinning at, Dad?"

"You. Home." His daughter sat in the seat closest to him, her back to the rest of the kitchen. She smiled at him.

"Weird, huh?" She took a sip from her mug.

"Nope." He reached out and held her hand. His baby girl. "Nice. Makes me feel settled in my soul." Letting go, he picked up his mug and brought it to his lips.

Tana cocked her head to the side, pulled the cup down from her face, but held it in her hands. "Then why aren't you sleeping?"

"Why, indeed." Dave laughed at his daughter's directness. Without a doubt, she was Millie's child. He studied her face before he answered her, determining how direct he needed to be with her, and chose to be an open book. He set the mug back on the table. "Because, my sweet daughter, there is a man in this house—a man who loves you more than I think you realize." The thought made Tana blush slightly, and maybe, Dave thought, even smile behind the mug warming her hands.

"And that's a problem?"

"Nope. Well . . ." He hesitated a bit.

"Ah, that is a problem."

"No. No in and of itself, it is not. In and of itself, it is a very good thing. What is a problem, is I am your father. I do still have a job to do." Tana giggled a little at her dad's tenderness toward her. He wanted nothing more than to protect her in some way. In any way he could. "And I intend to do it to the best of my ability."

"Just tell me you will go easy on him, Daddy."

"No, ma'am." He grinned at his daughter. "Any boy who intends to date, and maybe even marry . . ."

"Oh, Dad, we are a long way from talking marriage."

"Are you? I'm not so sure Tate's mind is a long way from it."

"What on earth did you guys talk about out there today?" she quizzed her dad.

"Nothing serious." She cocked her head at him again. "I promise." Dave picked up his mug and took a drink. "However, I see how he looks at you."

"Oh, Dad—"

"Don't 'oh, Dad' me. I'm serious." Their eyes locked, and Tana knew there was more than just a father worried about a boy in her life going on here. "And as much as your Momma and I want to see you in a loving relationship, and someday a 'happy ever after,' I'm not going just to let you go off with a guy without knowing him much better than I do."

"Meaning you need to know what his beliefs are about Jesus."

"That. Yes. And more." He watched as Tana seemed to study the liquid in her mug. "Baby." She lifted her head at his tender tone. "You have been through more than enough for a lifetime. I intend to make sure you are cared for by anyone I give your hand to."

Tana laughed again. "Now you sound like Tate."

"Do I?" Dave smiled at his daughter. "Well, it's good to know he is aware of the task ahead; that's a point in his favor." Tana's smile began to fade as she lost herself in her tea again. Dave could tell something else was stirring her soul. "Ya know, as much as I am enjoying this conversation, I don't believe you came down here to talk about my need to grill your boyfriend. What's keeping you awake tonight, sweet girl?"

She smiled softly at his ability to pin her down. She wondered how he could know her so well and still, she felt so lost and unknown. "You know, you and Mom have talked about Jesus so often, and yet, I still don't understand." Dang tears. "What am I missing, Daddy?"

"Missing?"

"Yes, missing. To struggle with believing as you do. I am clearly missing something in the translation of my reality and yours."

"Oh, I don't think you are missing anything, sweetheart. I think you know the truth." Dave held his daughter's gaze for a few moments. He loved seeing his wife's eyes looking back at him from his daughter's sweet face. "However, I do think you need to stop blaming yourself for what happened."

Tana was taken aback for a moment. "Blaming myself? How do you figure?"

Now it was Dave's turn to lose himself in his mug, the drink now almost cold. "You always seem to hold yourself back a bit. Like you have to be extra careful in each step you take, for fear of screwing something else up." Dave lifted his eyes to catch hers again. "When the reality is you didn't screw anything up in the first place. What happened to you was not your fault. You did nothing to make it happen."

Tana started to object, "Dad, I let go; I chased after the balloons; I ran into the crowd—"

He stopped her short. "Yes. And your mom and I didn't watch you close enough, or follow fast enough, or hold you tight enough. Baby, we can all play *what if* and *if only* games for the rest of our lives—and be miserable."

He slowed enough for his words to sink in. "Or . . ." He reached out and placed his hand over hers. "We can acknowledge our lives were turned upside down in a heartbeat a very long time ago. We can acknowledge terrible things happened to you that never should happen to anyone, especially not a young, defenseless little child. Then, we can acknowledge there is a God who can take what was meant for very evil purposes and use it to bring good into this world, and for His glory."

It was here Tana stiffened and physically struggled, Dave noticed. "Please hear me well, child. I am in no manner saying God did this to you on purpose. Or that you have no control over your own life."

"What does that leave, Dad?" Swimming in the green of her eyes, Dave could almost physically feel the pain in her pleading. His heart hurt as much as it did all those years ago when his daughter was first missing. Pain as fresh as when his baby girl was ripped from his life and taken so very far from his protective arms, and he had no way to bring her back home. Swallowing the lump in his throat, Dave struggled to help her make sense of all she carried.

"Close your eyes for me a minute." Tana cocked her head in a questioning jester. "Please," he responded. Tana obliged him. "I want you to picture if you will, a little girl, playing quietly in her living room. She's doing what children do, not misbehaving or getting out of control. Mom and Dad are sitting nearby, maybe having coffee, and chatting. The child is not out of their care, but neither is she their full attention."

He studied his daughter's face as she built the scene in her mind. He could see so much of her mother in her sweet face. He could also see the physical scars on that same face left by her captors so many years ago. "What is she doing?"

"She's following their footsteps and having a tea party with her dolls and stuffed animals." Dave smiled at her picture and could almost see, in his mind, Tana as a child doing the same thing.

"Perfect! Now, in the midst of all of that sweetness charges a cat being chased by a big, muddy dog. They are running full speed and trample right through her tea party. Cups are scattered and broken, the dolls—especially her favorite one—are torn, muddied, and scattered. The cat, claws extended as it's trying to get away, catches her legs, leaving her with long, bleeding cuts."

"Dad!" Her eyes flew open, the anguish a reaction to his verbal destruction.

Dave's voice remained calm and steady, despite the pleading in hers. "Is all of this damage the little girl's fault for playing on the floor?"

"No, of course not."

"Is it her parents for letting her play with the tea set?"

"No."

"Is it the dog's for chasing the cat?"

"Well . . . maybe, but that is what dogs do."

"Right. So now what?" He searched her eyes for a connection to his picture. "What does she need to do now?"

"She needs to let her folks comfort her."

"And the toys?"

"Well, I guess she needs to take them to her parents and let them fix what can be fixed and trash what can't."

"Right. She has a choice. She can sit in the midst of the destruction and cry, or she can go to her parents and trust them to make wise and helpful decisions." Tana watched his face as he explained his thoughts to her. "See, in this scenario, you would be the little girl, and God would be the parents. And you have sat in the middle of the destruction for long enough. Now, it's time to let God fix what He can and get rid of what isn't needed."

"And what exactly does that look like, Dad? How does one ask God to fix anything?"

"Well, baby doll, you start by asking God to forgive you of your sins—"

Tana stiffened again and interrupted her dad, "I thought you said I wasn't to blame."

"You aren't. But that doesn't make you blameless. We are all sinners. Every one of us. And in that, we must all ask God to forgive us for our sins. For the hate we carry. For the anger we carry. For trying to fix things on our own. Sweetheart, you have harbored your hatred of people and yourself for far too long. It's time to ask Him to forgive you for that choice and to help you make new choices."

Tana dropped her head. "I don't know how. I don't know if I can."

Dave reached across the table and took his daughter's hands in his own, "Let me pray with you, baby doll."

Chapter 11

Georgia, 2018

Once they found their way to the boat, Dave and Tate loaded it with poles, bait, sandwiches, and idle chit chat. Tate felt like he had known Dave his whole life, this sweet teddy bear of a man. He found himself drawn to Dave's calm, gentle spirit. His precise, almost mechanical movements while getting the boat ready, pushing off the shore and searching for fish, and the tender care of his wife was a fascinating dichotomy in Tate's mind. To see a man go through his tasks with so little emotion, and yet be so caring, even under so much stress, was impressive to the younger man.

After fishing in silence for a while, Tate began to seek some answers from the older generation. "I've gotta ask, Dave, how did you do it? How did you and your wife keep your marriage together in the middle of such turmoil?"

"How, indeed. I can honestly say it was not easy. We had our good days; we had our bad. We had days we thought we would never get through. Sometimes, we would go to bed thinking, 'I'm scared to go to sleep because then I will have to admit that this day, this event, actually happened,' and then the day would break on a new one, and, somehow, there was new courage to face it all again."

Dave reeled in his line, set it, and sent the bait flying across the lake while he contemplated the rest of his answer. "You know, son, grief is a funny thing. One might think you can love and experience joy and know what life is about. But, you don't. Not until you have walked the depths of pain, sorrow, and grief."

"How so?"

"I imagine you might know some of this personally; though, being so young when you lost your parents, you might not fully understand the difference. See, until you have walked in the cold, shadowy mist that is grief, you never really know what it's like to walk in the warm light of the sun."

Tate pondered the older man's thoughts. "You know, sir, I think for me, it's the opposite. Until Tana came into my life, I had no idea how dark, cold, and gray my world had been."

Tate watched as Dave surveyed his line dancing on the horizon, the water swallowing most of it into depths unknown. Gentle waves rolled past the entry point as if the lure had never intruded upon the surface, had never cracked it open. Tate wondered if the older man's heart was like the water—cracking, allowing things in, only to swallow them whole and appear completely untouched by the situation.

"She has ushered in such joy in my soul. I never knew the sunshine could be so warm or colors so bright before I met her. Even as Tana tried to push me away, I knew I would do whatever it took to be closer to her. To hold her close to me."

The silence hung in the air like the lures they cast, making Tate squirm in his skin more than his seat. Dave contemplated the younger man's words, aware of, though not acknowledging, his discomfort.

The sound of Dave's words when he finally spoke plopped into Tate's heart much like the lure would hit the water. "That's pretty big, son."

"I know it is, sir. And while I'm only now beginning to learn about and understand all she has been through, it only makes me love her more. She is strong. And she manages to be tender. I love the fight in her and her desire to protect those who cannot protect themselves. I love the way she traces her scar when she's feeling uncomfortable. I love her smile and being able to make her laugh. I love how she bites her lip when she's feeling vulnerable . . ."

As Dave brought in his line, he turned to face the young man. "And do you think she feels the same about you?"

"Honestly, sir, I'm not always sure. She has not fully let down her guard. And I get that. She has been through much, faced hurt, and been abused." Staring out over the water, Tate figured now, while they were on the subject of this man's daughter, he needed to put his heart out there. He needed to be as open and clear with this man as possible. "It is my desire to make sure that never happens again. It is my desire to spend the rest of my life making sure she knows how amazing she is."

"What exactly are you saying?"

"I'm telling you I am in love with Tana." Tate swallowed hard, realizing he was more nervous than he anticipated. Turning to face Dave while taking a deep breath, he said, "I'm asking your permission to ask her to marry me. Now, I know she isn't ready yet, and I will not rush that. But I wanted to ask you face to face so that when she is, I can be ready to ask her."

"You know marriage is not easy under the best circumstances. There is nothing about Montana's life that has been the best circumstance. It may be the 'Promise Land,' but there are giants in that land that will need to be removed."

"Yes, sir. I feel like one at a time; we can take them on together. Alone, we will never make it, but together, we can be strong."

Dave studied the young man's face hard, the strong chin, steel blue eyes, the dark hair agitated by the wind. He then turned slowly, deliberately back toward the edge of the boat, and let his line fly back into the water. Tate couldn't tell if the rocking of the boat was making his stomach do flips, or if it was Dave's silence.

As Tate tried to calm his nerves, he noticed a sly smile forming on Dave's lips. Ah, that's where Tana gets it. Dave leaned back in his chair and faced him. "Tate, I would be happy to have you as a son-in-law, and I know Millie would be thrilled. However, I need to know one thing first."

Relieved, Tate asked, "What is that, sir?"

"Where do you stand with Jesus?"

"Jesus? Well, my aunt and uncle are believers, but I don't know. I've always struggled with the concept of an all-powerful God controlling all that goes on in life. I guess I believe he was a good man, a good teacher. Why? Does that matter?"

"If you are going to lead a family, then yes, it matters. If you only believe He was a good man, your mistake is that you don't know the Scriptures and the power of God. My challenge to you would be this: before you ever ask any woman to marry you, you need to know Jesus personally. There is no other way to make a marriage work."

"And what does that mean to you, knowing Jesus personally? I mean it's not like I can walk up to Him and shake His hand."

"No, I suppose you cannot do that. Knowing Jesus is more about knowing the heart of who Jesus is, talking to Him in prayer, finding your comfort and strength in His Spirit."

"So I ask to know Him, and He suddenly takes over my life?"

"Ha, no. It's not like that at all. The Bible is a book, but it is also alive. When you study the Bible, you will find it studies you. As you read about the things Jesus did, the words He said, you begin to understand His heart. But you also begin to understand your own heart. There is darkness found in every man. The hatred people have for one another."

"I thought that's what it meant to be a religious person, hating those who are not like you."

"Is that how you see your aunt and uncle?"

"Gosh, no. They are just normal people."

"But they believe in Jesus?"

"Yes."

"That tells me you allow the media to color your opinion of who Jesus is more than your own experience with people who follow him."

"I guess I've never thought much about it."

"Maybe it's time you did."

Washington, DC, 2017

The spring breeze tossed her hair into her coffee cup. After tucking the rogue strand behind her ear a third time, Tana began doubting the choice of waiting at an outside table as much as she questioned her decision to meet Tate at all. Between the few times she had run into him, all of the ignored voicemail messages, and the six dozen roses he sent to her house, she felt like this conversation would be the only way to fully rid herself of his attempts to chat with her. The one snag was young Greg Blakely. If that child was in half the trouble it sounded like he was in . . .

"Hi!" the sound came from behind, the voice as deep as it was cheery. He quickly circled to the front of her seat, placed his order number on the tabletop, and pulled out the chair, "Do you mind?"

She shook her head. "That's why you are here, right?"

His grin sparkled as much as his blue eyes. "It is." Tate sat back into the seat, watching the dark-haired beauty before him. Without so much as a word, she stole his breath and wrapped him into a knot. He wondered if he had ever been this nervous in college?

Before Tana could say anything else, the waitress stepped in, "White chocolate mochaccino?"

"That's mine," Tate answered with a soft smile as his eyes caught her name tag. "Thank you, Barbara Jean. I appreciate you bringing it over."

Her cheeks flushed at the unexpected sound of her name. "Of course. Do you need anything else?" Barbara Jean asked them as she tried to remove the plastic number from its temporary home.

"Not at this time," he told her as he reached out to steady the stand, allowing the number to pull free. "I appreciate it."

"Enjoy," she flashed a grin and hustled back toward the counter.

Tana couldn't decide if she was amused or irritated by the interaction she just witnessed. Her comment topics felt wide open, though not all would prove valuable. She settled on his coffee choice. "A coffee lightweight, huh?"

"That obvious?"

"A mochaccino?" Tana raised an eyebrow as she spoke, "That's just a half step away from a child's hot chocolate."

Tate chuckled. "Hot chocolate, huh? Well, what do you recommend?"

"I would suggest at least a cappuccino. You know, espresso and both steamed and frothed milk. Shoot, you could even add the chocolate shavings on top if you wanted that."

Tate took a tentative sip from his hot cup before he settled on a question for the beauty across the table. "I am new to coffee. Somehow I made it through law school on nothing stronger than soda. So how is a cappuccino different from what I have?"

"Mostly in the espresso instead of coffee." When there was not much of a response from Tate, Tana continued, "You know, the strength of the hot, dark liquid used to create the beverage you are consuming."

Once more, he studied her. Attention to detail proved strong. Tate hoped that would be a tremendous help for his case. Again, he smiled at her. "I'll give it a shot next time—no pun intended." He chuckled for a moment. When Tana failed to join his laughter, he cleared his throat and moved to the topic at hand. "I asked to meet you because my uncle said your specialty is kids in trouble. Specifically, trafficked kids."

Placing the cup on top of the table, Tana gave him an abrupt, "He's not wrong."

"Good. Then I have a case I would like some help with."

Georgia, 2018

Tana woke the next morning feeling lighter than she could ever remember. What was this she felt? Could there really be a joy in her spirit? She relished in the conversation with her father. Her love for that man was growing every day. Making her way to the kitchen, she found herself humming, though she really couldn't put her finger on what the song was.

Stepping into the kitchen, she found her mom sitting at the table, coffee steaming from the mug in front of her, her Bible open beside the cup. Tana laughed at the sight of her mom in almost the same place and position her dad had been. The coffee maker kept the pot warm, and the low flicker of the flame under the tea kettle popped gently to its own beat on the stove.

"Good morning, darling," Millie called, looking up from her reading. "I wasn't sure if you would want to start with coffee or tea this morning."

"Good morning, Mom. Coffee will do nicely, thank you, but you don't have to get up." Millie was moving faster than Tana could get the words out of her mouth. "Mom, I can pour my own coffee," she said as she laughed gently.

Millie smiled as she handed her a cup. "Of this, I have no doubt. However, I do not often have the chance to serve my sweet daughter these days and would appreciate you not taking that pleasure from me."

Tana bowed her head slightly as she accepted the cup. "Yes, ma'am." Then she leaned over and gently kissed her mother's warm, soft cheek.

"Ah, thank you very much." Mille also tipped her head. "Shall we enjoy the warm sun outside?"

"That would be lovely!" Together they made their way to the table on the back porch. As the ladies moved from the cool air conditioning to the warmth of the Georgia morning sun, the crisp air echoed the feeling of the fresh life Tana felt inside. The only sound was of the birds darting from tree to ground and back as they searched for their breakfast. And their joyous songs of celebration. Tana found the whole picture rather glorious this morning. "Do you remember Dr. Stoltenberg?"

Millie pondered the question briefly. "From your college? Yes, I believe so."

"We had a long conversation last night. Did you know she is a Christian?"

"Really? I don't believe I knew that." She took another sip, not wanting to allow her hopes to rise too high.

"Yep. I think I felt it, even though I couldn't tell you that's why I was drawn to her. And that's one of the reasons she has always kept tabs on me; she felt like God asked her to. Anyway, it seems forgiveness is the theme for the weekend." Tana watched her mom for a bit then continued. "She feels there is something she called the mercy of forgiveness I need to learn to walk in." Tana played with her cup absently, running her finger around the edge. "If I had to guess, that is probably what you were learning to walk in with Jack."

Millie nodded her head. "That sounds about right."

"I know these things take time, but I don't really want it to take me years and years to learn." Tana looked up at her mom. "I wrestled with our conversation for a while. Then I got up and came downstairs and ran into Dad." Tana took a sip of her coffee. She allowed the warmth to ease into her body. "We talked about so much." Millie was pretty sure she could see a twinkle in Tana's eyes. "He's a very wise man."

"This I know." Millie smiled back at her daughter over the rim of her coffee cup.

Tana smiled at her mom's pleasure in who Dave was as a man. "I'm sure you do. So anyway, long story short, I wanted to let you know, I took a step toward that end by asking Jesus to forgive me last night."

At this news, Millie let out an excited, "Praise You, Jesus!"

Chapter 12

Georgia, 2018

Lamenting a much too quick trip, Dave and Millie watched as Tana and Tate entered the rental car and pulled out of their driveway. "I think he's a good guy, Millie."

"I don't disagree, Dave." Millie turned back and walked through their front door. "But is he the right guy?"

Following his wife into the house Dave gave a voice to his thoughts. "I don't know, sweetheart. Time will tell, I suppose." Once they returned the car, Tate and Tana made their way to the gate and quickly settled into their seats on the plane.

The ride back to DC found Tate deeply in thought and Tana more relaxed than he'd ever known her. His mind wandered from conversations with Dave and Tana to trying to win her over the first time. In his mind's eye, he could picture the office and looking out the glass front to see her walking toward the elevator. It was the first time he'd seen her since that day in the courtroom. He ran to the door and started down the hall.

"Well, hi there, stranger. I was just headed to walk my uncle's next appointment at the office, thinking I should get outside more. I need more sunshine in my life. And here you are, bringing the sunshine and light with you."

Tana jumped at the sound of his voice as he walked up behind her while she waited for the elevator. She turned to face him—with her amazing green eyes. Tate felt his knees weaken.

"Well, that was quite the line, Mr. . . ." Trying to be icy and standoffish, her voice was still silky smooth. Yeah, he was toast, and he knew it.

"It's Tate. Tate Palmer. We met a few weeks back." Fifteen, he thought, but who's counting? "You know I have been thinking about you. You left an impression on me."

"Oh? Like a shoe?"

"Ha. Funny girl. Nope. Like you were amazing to watch on the stand. Mesmerizing even." *Maybe a hint of a smile there or just a bit of blush in her cheeks?* "Look, I know this is a bit forward, but I really would like to get to know you better. I left a couple of messages. . . . I can't ever seem to catch you on the phone."

"Yeah. Sorry. I've been busy."

Tate laughed. "So I've noticed. How about grabbing a coffee this afternoon?"

"Wow. That's so kind. I was just leaving. Maybe next time."

"Hmmm." The elevator doors slid open, and there stood Belmont. Tate noticed how Tana seemed to stiffen as soon as she saw him, and he wondered why. Tate greeted him, "Ah, Belmont. Nice timing. I just came down to find you." He turned to find Tana stepping into the elevator, "Okay. Next time. But then it will be up to dinner because you keep avoiding me."

She turned around to see him standing at the threshold, Belmont impatiently waiting on him, and as the doors slid shut, she said, "Good luck catching me."

Tate stood there for a few minutes. He wished he could be there when they delivered the flowers, now that he had run into her. He hadn't planned that little nuance, but he liked what it might make her think. He looked at Belmont. "Uncle Lee is waiting."

The memory made him laugh a bit louder than he intended. Tana turned in her seat to face him, "Care to share what you're laughing about?"

"I just remembered my first attempts at talking you into going out with me."

"Oh, my . . . You did try hard," she smiled at him. The memories flooded her mind. "The roses were a nice touch."

"That was a nice touch, wasn't it? I knew you would be mine then."

"What? No way. You were sweating bullets until I finally agreed to go out with you—"

"Yes, yes I was . . ." He laughed again. "It was good because you accepted because I wasn't sure how I was going to up the ante after sending you six dozen roses."

"Each dozen with one word on the card. Lucky for you I'm not allergic to roses!"

"Oh, man, that would have been bad. But they got you to call me back."

"Well, the roses, and our conversation by the elevator with the Blakely case kicker. How did you time that so well?"

"Luck was totally on my side that day, my darling. Totally on my side."

Tana leaned over and kissed him. "Nope. It was totally on my side." She leaned back into her seat, still facing him, thoughts stirring in her heart and mind. Tana settled on a direction of conversation as she asked Tate, "Do you remember talking about Mom praying for someone to watch over me while I was with the traffickers?"

"Of course."

"I had a conversation with a former professor of mine a couple days ago. I now agree with you."

Tate raised an eyebrow. "Oh, yeah?"

"Yeah. And I took a big step while talking with Dad." She took a breath and plunged into the truth without giving Tate a chance to question her. "I asked Jesus to forgive me and be my savior."

"Forgive you? For what?"

"Well, there's much too that, but let's start with this . . . my bitterness was a sin. Not that it just all vanished, but I feel so much more joy now. More than I've ever felt—well, at least more than I ever remember feeling." She let the words sink in a bit before she added, "I don't know where you are with Jesus, but I wanted to let you know where I am."

"That's funny. Your Dad wanted to know the same thing, and I didn't know how to answer him." He sat back in his seat and looked straight ahead. "I still don't, if I'm being honest."

Washington, DC, 2018

Lee called Tate into his office as soon as he got in on his first morning back. "Sorry I missed you at home this morning." He motioned for Tate to sit down.

"We got in late last night, and I'm moving a bit slowly this morning."

"Did you have a good trip?"

Tate grinned, warmed by the afterglow of their adventure. "Yes. I cannot wait to tell you and Nini about it over dinner tonight."

"Fabulous." Lee hesitated a bit. "I just got off the phone with the DA from Georgia. We are being asked to look into a case I don't have time for, and I need to know if you can handle it, boy."

Boy. Tate was growing to hate that word. Why did his uncle still look at him as a boy? "I don't even know what that means. Since when do you question my ability, Uncle Lee?'

"It's not your ability I question, boy." Tate was a little shocked at the strength of his uncle's reaction. "I know you are one of the best lawyers around, no there is no question of you being able to fight this case. It's your emotional involvement." Tate could feel the blank stare on his face. Lee, unfazed by his nephew's indignantly silent reply, said, "Look, I know you are personally involved with Tana. And a guy is being brought up from Georgia who has a connection to her history. I have not looked at his file; there is just too much going on. Since you have knowledge of that history, and I don't, I need to know you can question him without letting your emotions rule you."

"Emotions? You are worried about emotions? What about conflict of interest?"

"What conflict? You aren't prosecuting him, just interviewing him. Gathering information. I just don't want you to be hotheaded."

Tate snickered. "Hotheaded? When have I ever been? Of course, I can interview him." Tate took a breath and asked, "Why now? I mean why not earlier?"

"New information. He's been in the system for years, the DA down there says he was arrested for child porn, and then he confessed to kidnapping Montana, but now claims to have some more information he's willing to share. I'm not sure it isn't too late for him to help us with anything, but I need you to go see what he knows."

"In the system for years? And you've never talked to him before?"

"Nope. This is the first time I've been handed his case. He's been in the Georgia prison system since he was originally arrested. The sheriff there says he has some serious allegations to discuss with us. I guess he asked for our office by name. They are going to email the reports, and all photos will be shipped to our office. Right now, I just need someone to talk to him and determine if we can use what he has at all."

"Yes, sir. I will handle it."

"Good. I had hoped that would be your answer, so I gave them your email address. You should be receiving that file today."

Tate started to walk back to his office and thought better of it. "Hey, Uncle Lee?" His eyes locked with the older man's. "I'm going to let Tana know this is going on so she's not blindsided by any of this."

Lee contemplated the idea. "That's probably a very wise move young man."

As Tana rounded the final corner of her jog, her phone rang. She kicked up her pace to get to her doorway before she stopped to see who was calling. When she saw Tate's picture staring back at her, she was quick to answer it. "You know you are interrupting my run, right?"

"The sound of your voice makes me very happy; you don't have to be breathing heavy just for me," he teased. He hesitated for just a second. "Actually I need to let you know what just came across my desk."

She dug out her key and let herself into the apartment. "Okay; I'm putting you on speaker." She set the phone on the counter and headed to the fridge for a bottle of water. "What's going on."

"I know you don't like to talk about your history, so this may be a difficult conversation for you."

Setting the bottle down, Tana stared into the phone, like she was trying to make eye contact with Tate. She asked him, "What does that mean, Tate?"

With another deep breath, Tate answered, "Jack Beacher is offering information on the trafficking ring. They are currently moving him from Georgia to DC, and he has asked to talk directly with our office."

"Why? Why would he do that?" she wondered out loud. "I mean, why would they ask for your office?"

"I honestly have no idea. However, I think I'm about to find out. Lee has more than he wants on his docket, and he asked me to talk to

Jack. I just wanted you to know ahead of time; this is going down." Tana did not answer him. "Hey? You still there?"

"Yeah," she slowly answered. "I guess I always knew this was a possibility. I don't know that I ever really expected it to come up." She hesitated again. "Nor did I every expect it to come across your desk."

"Does that bother you?"

"Well, I don't know. I mean, it's probably one thing to hear the details from me. It's probably another to read and hear the full, sterile, emotionless detail from a court case—or the details from the man himself."

Tate thought he sensed her hesitation. "Montana. I need you to hear me right now."

"I'm listening." She could feel the tears coming. Again.

"You are the only woman I want. Nothing any of these people have to say would change that for me."

"I hear the words you are saying. I—I just . . ." Tana took a deep breath to regain control of her emotions. "I just don't want you to ever look at me and see the images of a battered, damaged little girl."

"Oh, darling. You are not that little girl anymore. You are my beautiful, strong, wide open Montana Grace. No one could ever make me see anything less or different from that. I promise you that. Okay?"

She wiped the tears from her face. "Okay."

"Now, I know this may be tough, but I think it might be wise for you to give the light version to Lee and Sonja tonight so they know what is coming."

She sighed a little. "You are probably right—again."

Laughing, he teased her one more time. "I'm always right, baby!" With a more serious tone, he added, "I love you, beautiful. Always."

"I love you, too, charming. Always." Each beat of her heart announced the truth in those words. Then, resting her head on the phone, she closed her eyes and listened to the song her heart was singing.

Bump, bump. I do. Bump, bump. Love you. Bump, bump.

Tana had never felt the emotion flowing through her veins like right at that moment. She had an ugly story to tell and could only pray it didn't drive the man or his family away.

Tate hung up the phone and made his way to the office library to research a few cases for the morning.

When Tate sat at his desk after lunch, he checked his email. Nervous? Excited? He wasn't sure anymore. Montana's history, his precious Tana, was wrapped up like a package for him to open. Maybe he could begin to understand. Maybe he could help her understand. Help her heal. Yes. Healing. That's what she needed.

He slowly lifted the cover and began to read the details of abduction, torture, and abuse. All the scars, the emotions such young children should never have to carry. And there were more than just Tana. There seemed to be something bigger this guy was part of. However, once he was caught, he only confessed to her abduction and trafficking and took his prison time.

Jack Beacher. He said it out loud. Let the name roll off his tongue. The more he read, the deeper he allowed the hatred, of these men and the life they lead, to burrow into every cell of his body. He began to grow a deeper appreciation for all Tana did every day. Helping other little girls out of the trauma she had lived through takes grit. There was also a special hate born for Jack Beacher. The man who started a lifetime of nightmares for Tana. He tenderly offered to help a four-year-old find her parents and whisked her off into an inky black night eight years long. That hate was a chasm in Tate's heart, separating good and evil. At the same time, the love and desire to protect this woman grew. Each word seared the sting of his tears like a brand on his face.

Tate clicked on one of the links in the email. Ugh. Would IT ever get this issue with graphics taken care of? He leaned over the computer to face the door. "Hey, Joy, get IT up here. This stupid computer isn't bringing up photos again. I can't get any of the photos from this file to load."

"Yes, Mr. Palmer."

Chapter 13

Washington, DC, 2018

The aroma coming from his kitchen was a welcome comfort. Walking in to find his beautiful wife busy at the stove surrounded by what looked like either the aftermath of Thanksgiving dinner or an invasion of a teenage football team was a surprising sight for a weeknight. Dishes, pots, and pans had been haphazardly scattered across the usually immaculate kitchen. Lee silently watched Sonja mixing, adding, and concocting in such a fluid motion, it was almost a mesmerizing dance of love she was performing. To not startle her when she finally turned around, he gently said, "It smells amazing in here."

"Hi, babe!" She spun around, grinning from ear to ear. "I didn't hear you pull up."

"Are we having a dinner party I forgot about?" He gathered his wife in his arms and pulled her close to him.

"More like one you didn't know about." She reached up and kissed him hello. "Tate called me this afternoon and asked if he could bring Tana for dinner. I guess he wants her to talk to us about her past a little tonight. I don't know why."

"I think I do."

"Well, I'm not sure I care why. I'm just glad to get to know her a little better. I mean, if he wants to marry her, I think spending time with her is a fantastic idea!"

"Yes, I suppose it is."

Sensing his hesitation, Sonja studied his face, aged over the years, though maybe faster in the last couple. His deep blue eyes were always her favorite feature. Even with the storm brewing behind them making them more sea green, she loved to get lost in them. "I'm guessing we will be up late talking tonight. However, I would appreciate you wiping the scowl from your sweet face before Tate and Tana arrive."

"Wow, am I that obvious?"

"Like an open book." She grinned at him. Once again he leaned in and kissed his wife. "What was that for?"

"I'm ridding myself of a nasty scowl my amazing wife informed me was on my face."

"What a fabulous idea! However, I need to finish getting dinner ready, so why don't you go change and help me set the table?"

"Yes, ma'am."

Los Angeles, 2017

Lee, Tate, and Tana gathered around the speakerphone on Lee's desk, collectively willing the phone to ring. Pen in hand and paper in front of him, Lee questioned for the fourth time, "What time did Chuck say he would call?"

"He said ten. Maybe he's stuck in traffic," Tate wondered.

Tana was unimpressed by the two men. "You guys are a bit uptight. LA time is always fifteen minutes behind everyone else."

Before Tana's final syllable faded into the air, the phone vibrated to life with a loud ring. Tate jumped up, pushing the talk button and nearly spilling Lee's coffee in the process. Grabbing the tilting cup, Lee answered, "This is Lee Palmer." Silence. "Hello?"

A timid voice responded, "Uh, I was looking for a Mr. Tate Palmer."

Leaning close to the speaker, Tate spoke up, "Hi! I'm Tate. Are you Greg?"

"Ya."

"That's great. I have here with me, Lee, who you already spoke to, and Tana."

"Hi, Greg!" Tana smiled, hoping Greg could feel the warmth through the phone.

"Hi."

Tate went on, "They are both very good at handling situations like yours. Can you tell me who is with you, Greg?"

"Um, Mr. Chuck, my mom, and me. That's it."

Keeping the conversation moving, Tate offered, "It's nice to meet you all over the phone. Especially you, Greg. Chuck told me you are a great kid."

Silence.

"Hey, buddy, I know this is a very hard subject to talk about," Lee tried. "How about we just start asking questions, and you can tell us what you don't want to answer. Okay?"

"Okay."

"When you went home, did you tell your mother what had happened?"

Greg hesitated before answering, "No."

"Why not?"

"I was scared."

"I bet you were. Can you tell me what happened?"

"I went to bed."

Lee smiled. "I mean, before you got home."

157

"Oh." Greg swallowed, his fingers fighting with a pen on Chuck's desk. "I went to a party."

"Who's party?"

Greg paused, his eyebrows furrowed and his lips sunk into a deep frown. "I can't remember. Stan said it was for some big hair, um . . . wait. No. That's not right."

Lee tried to help. "Do you mean big wigs, son?"

"Yeah! That's it. Big wigs in Hollywood and politics."

"And what happened at the party?" Tate jumped into the conversation.

"It was loud and smokey. I didn't like being around all those people, so I went outside and looked for a basketball."

Tana jumped in and asked, "Were you alone?"

"Yeah. Until Stan came outside."

"Stan did?" Tana questioned, glancing at Tate and Lee.

"Yeah. He found the ball for me."

"And then what happened?"

Chuck and Silvia encouraged Greg to continue. "We played HORSE until Stan started talking."

"What did he talk about?"

"Well, at first it was about my dad. But then he started talking about seeing an old man's body and . . ." Greg hesitated, trying to find words he didn't really have. He settled for nondescript, hoping they wouldn't push for more. "Other things. And that's when Stan's dad showed up."

Lee encouraged Greg to go on. "And what happened?"

Greg continued to explain what happened the night—that Stan pushed him up against the tree—in details no ten-year-old child should understand, let alone experience. Lee cringed, his stomach turning at the idea of what this boy had been through.

Lee repeated Greg's words softly and paused, feeling the blood pounding against his temples. Then he asked Greg to clarify, "Who did this?"

"Stan and his dad."

"Greg, you have been so brave, son. Thank you for talking with us today. Can you put Mr. Blue back on the phone please?"

"Yes, sir."

"This is Chuck."

"Hey, Chuck. Man, this definitely sounds like something we need to look into more. Do you know if there are any other kids we can talk to regarding Stan and his dad?"

Chuck bristled, "You need more?"

Tana offered him some comfort. "I know that's hard to understand, but people have had trouble before. So we need to build a case consisting primarily of three witnesses and at least two pieces of physical evidence. We will need the main victim in the case and two similar fact witnesses."

"Why is it so important to have three children?"

"Well, that's what we have learned from these other cases." Lee breathed out a deep sigh, willing the truth not to get to his heart again. His will faltered as he spoke just above a whisper. "In the past, the jurors didn't believe the one child."

Tana admitted, "So if you have multiple witnesses essentially testifying to the same thing—"

For the moment, Chuck fully understood what they were telling him. "It adds to the credibility." His gut clenched as the facts settled. "What you are telling me is for Greg to be believed, other children had to have had the same experience with Stan and his father."

Once more, a sigh escaped Lee's lips, followed by the words, "Yes. As awful as that is, it is correct."

Washington, DC, 2018

The drive through DC always proved to be a bit chaotic, though Tate was thoroughly aware Tana was unfazed by any of the traffic during this half-hour trip from her condo on 34th in Georgetown to Alexandria and the house his aunt and uncle owned on Southdown Road. Not that she was ever a backseat driver, but more like she was usually very savvy and watched everything around her. Tonight, she tripped down memory lane and lost herself in a traumatic world.

Tate reached out and gently took her hand. She held it without looking at him. "You doing okay, babe?"

She watched a few more trees and a glimpse or two of water pass by before responding, "Yes." She turned toward him, smiled faintly, and gripped his hand a little tighter. "Yes, I'm fine. A bit nervous, I suppose. The concept of telling a man I've only worked with and a woman I've never met everything I've been through makes me sick to my stomach. As much as I want to get to know the incredible people who raised such an amazing man, this is not the way I wanted to go about it."

She turned back to the window. "I feel like once again Jack has me in a place I don't honestly want to be, where once again I have little control over what happens in my life." She quickly turned back toward Tate. "And before you suggest we don't have to do this, that is not where I'm going with what I'm saying."

Tate smiled. "Am I that predictable?"

Tana met his grin with a more pronounced one of her own, despite the tear sliding down her cheek. Without letting go of her hand, Tate reached up and used the back of his hand to wipe it away. "I know they need to know. I just would have liked for them to see me for who I am now, not who I was . . ."

"They will see you for who you are, a strong woman who has risen above all she was handed, with amazing grace and dignity. They will see you as the beautiful woman you are."

They pulled up the driveway as the beauty of the area over-whelmed Tana. The slight breeze rustling the trees, the smell of rain in the air, the sight of the Potomac as it bounced along its borders. "This is a fantastic place!"

"Like your folks' place isn't?"

"Ha. No, not at all. I'm just saying this is a beautiful place. I mean, I love Georgia, but my heart is here in DC. It's like a slower New York with a heaping helping of Southern hospitality. There is nothing like it anywhere else. I find being so close to the water such a comfort. That's part of why I chose my place. I love being able to walk down to Waterfront Park on Saturday mornings. Or grab a coffee before watching the rowing teams practice or race. There's just some-thing peaceful and settling about the water."

Tate grabbed her hand and lead her to the back of the house and a better view of the river. "Or the sun setting on the water?"

"Oh, yes. A sun setting over the water is almost perfection. Though technically, since we are on the west side of the river, it will be setting behind us."

Tate laughed with her. "Maybe we can get out here after dinner, and watch the sunset while sitting by the water."

"That would be lovely." They turned, and Tate led her up the stairs to the deck and into the house through the kitchen, where Sonja was putting last-minute touches on dinner.

"Tate!" she laughed and chastised him as she hugged him. "You were supposed to bring this young lady in through the front door, not through my messy kitchen."

"I'm sorry, Nini. We were talking about the water, and I wanted to show her the amazing view of the river you guys have. Want me to take her back out and around the house?"

"Nope. You already made the first impression." She turned to Tana. "For that, I must apologize. I thought I taught him better."

It was Tana's turn to laugh. "No harm, no foul. I promise all I see is a beautiful home with an amazing view. It's so incredibly peaceful here. I'm Tana." Tana offered her hand to shake Sonja's.

"Sonja Palmer." She took hold of Tana's hand and said, "I'm more of a hugger; do you mind?" Tana smiled and shook her head, letting Sonja pull her close for a quick hug. "I'm so very glad to meet you finally. I have heard amazing things from both Tate and Lee."

"He's very kind. You have raised an impressive young man, and your husband is a champion that I'm proud to work with."

"Thank you." Sonja smiled at Tate. "However, I really cannot take the credit for that. I think they are both just incredible."

As if on cue, Lee strolled into the kitchen. "Hey, I didn't know we were having the party in here. Welcome to our home, Tana." He also stepped in and gave her a quick squeeze. "Tate, good to see you." He gathered the boy in a playful bear hug, which seemed so out of character compared to the way Tana usually saw him, yet she could tell this was a ritual between these two guys. The bond was more than an uncle and nephew would have. Probably as close to father-son as you could be without actually being the father.

Tana turned back to Sonja. "Tate calls you Nini? How did that get started?" Sonja turned to face her, a smile on her face and a bowl of green beans in her hands. "Can I help at all?"

"Sure, would you take these to the table?"

"No, Nini, let me." Tate stepped into their conversation.

"Thank you." She turned from him back to Tana and smiled at her. "It was what his momma called me. So when he started talking, it came out pretty easily, and it stuck."

162

Chapter 14

Los Angeles, 2017

"How do we go about finding other kids?" Silvia paced Chuck's office floor. "I don't think I can send him to DC knowing what happened here."

"Honestly, I think that's a question for Tate and . . .Tana, was it?"

"I think so."

"Yeah, Tana." Chuck grabbed a notebook off of his desk, flipped a few pages, and picked up a pen. "Maybe our best bet is to make a list of the things we need to talk to them about?"

"Maybe. I just don't know. What about a psychologist?" Silvia continued to pace, her arms wrapped around her, trying to ward off a chill she continued to fight. "I mean, maybe there is—"

Greg squirmed around in his chair until he sat upright. "What about Mr. Wade?"

"—one most young actors use?" She stopped in her tracks as the boy's words settled in her ears. Slowly, she turned to face Greg. "What, son?"

"Mr. Wade. He knows all about lots of people. Maybe he would know something."

Silvia's eyes met Chuck's as they each processed the idea. Chuck spoke first, "Well. That's not a bad idea, Greg. I'll talk to Tate later tonight and see what he thinks."

Washington, DC, 2018

Memories of the previous night's dinner seem to be fading fast as he thought of his morning. Tate tried to steady his nerves as he made his way down the chilled corridor. With each step, he could almost feel the burning hate pulsing through his veins. Reading through the thick file told Tate that Jack was still a good five years away from being up for parole; yet here he was, offering new information on the traffickers he had worked with when he was on the streets.

It made him angry.

It disgusted him.

It fueled his hatred.

Honestly, in Tate's opinion, it was fifteen years too late for new information and any plea deal. More like twenty-three years too late—anything after Tana's abduction qualified as too late, in his opinion.

He absentmindedly wiped his clammy hands on his slacks as he walked the hall, switching his files and papers from one hand to the other. His thoughts collided in his brain like rocks in a tumbler, polishing the rage in his heart.

He reached the door and took a deep breath. The knob felt cold and slimy to his touch, so he brushed his hand on his pants again and took a firm grip. As the door flung open, his senses overloaded like water thrown on hot coals, etching the scene forever in his mind. The earth froze in place as he tried to process all he saw.

The face of the person seated before him was older, scarred, and weathered, the hair grayer. Shoulders thinner, more rounded. He was still muscular, in an old man sense. The eyes were not as bright as they once were. Still, it was undeniable. Generations were wrapped up in that face. Grandfather, to father, to son. Uncles and cousins too. Bloodlines run thick.

Tate could not breathe, wasn't sure he could stand, knew he couldn't move.

Composure. Tate needed to find it. He was about to confront the abductor of his girlfriend with the one person he never expected.

Because he was dead.

Had been dead for twenty-five years.

He was dead.

And yet . . . there he sat. At the table in his interrogation room. All the pictures Tate studied so often while growing up were fully alive and right in front of him. Living and breathing life. Tate was looking directly at him. And as he wrestled with making this new information fit into his puzzle, a voice exploded in his ear.

"Tate? Are you okay, son?"

Slowly Tate's head turned toward the noise.

Millie.

Millie was speaking to him.

Millie.

Millie was sitting in the room.

Millie.

Millie was talking with the man who abducted Montana.

Millie.

Millie was talking to his father.

"Ma'am." He felt his dry tongue scrape the roof of his mouth as it began to find words to answer her. "I did not expect to find you here this morning."

"Jack asked me to come pray with him."

Chapter 15

Los Angeles, 2017

Chuck paced the office floor. Waiting for Wade Bale was normal. Actors of his caliber were often late, looking to make a grand entrance for whatever they were going about doing. Photo shoots. Meet and greets. Dinners. Keeping the people waiting and wanting more seemed to be the goal.

The front door flew open, and a booming voice called out, "Chuckie. Chuckie. Chuckie."

"In my office, Wade." Chuck could only shake his head as he stopped behind his desk. Not many people got away with calling him Chuckie, but Wade could get away with just about anything. Wade Bale, and actors like him, paid the bills with all the head shots and promo shoots. Early in Wade and Chuck's careers, they hit a sweet spot and had worked together for almost a decade.

Wade Bale slid into his office and the chair in front of Chuck's desk in nearly one smooth move. He leaned back into the seat, crossing his ankle over his knee as Chuck also sat down. "Normally, it's me calling you for one of your fabulous photo shoots.

Not very often do you call me for a conversation. What's going on, ole buddy?"

Chuck hesitated. How does one even start this conversation? Hey! Have you ever been molested? Do you know anyone who has? Did anyone touch you in ways they shouldn't have? Nothing running through Chuck's mind felt kind or like he was doing anything less than invading the man's personal space.

"Wow, Chuckie. I've never known you to be at a loss for words. What's going on?"

Sighing, Chuck took a shot at starting. "You know Greg Blakely?"

"Yeah. Great kid."

"Did you know his mom works for me?"

Wade thought for a minute before the light flickered in his eyes. "Silvia? Greg is Silvia's kid? I mean, I know Renee doesn't have any kids."

"Yes, he's Silvia's son. What do you know about Stan West?"

The smile fell from Wade's face. "What are you looking for, Chuck?"

"Looking? Understanding, maybe."

"Understanding? Sounds like you are trying to open a can of worms you don't really want to open."

Chuck leaned forward in his chair. "Is that a threat, Wade?"

"Threat? No, buddy, that's a warning. I want to keep you safe, not hurt you."

"So instead you let a little boy get hurt?"

"What do you want from me, Chuck?"

"I want to know if what has happened to Greg has happened to others and if we can get them to testify to it."

"Oh, for sure whatever happened—and I don't want to know details—has happened to someone else. It's sort of a Hollywood rite of passage, or a not-talked-about secret everyone knows."

"I didn't know," Chuck growled.

"I'm sure you knew but didn't want to admit what you saw or heard was really that. You are a good guy, Chuck. You don't play in those games." Wade set both feet on the floor and stood up. "I don't know that you can get anyone to testify to what has happened to them. They would be afraid of losing a job or their status. If you want to keep working in this town, you keep your mouth shut."

"And destroy little kids along the way?"

"The price of fame, buddy. The price of fame." He turned to walk out of the office but stopped and faced Chuck. "For what it's worth, I'm sorry that happened to Greg. He really is a good kid. And does a great job. But you need to watch yourself. If you stir up a bunch of trouble for people like Stan West, you will start to lose jobs yourself."

Washington, DC, 2018

Running back down the hall, Tate threw open Lee's office door nearly before he reached it. "Tell me again what happened."

Looking up from his computer, Lee calmly answered, "What happened when?"

"How did my parents die?" he demanded.

Lee studied his nephew before he answered. Tate was now pacing the floor, mumbling something under his breath. Lee watched a moment before he questioned, "Why so agitated, boy?"

"Just tell me, Lee!" Tate was nearly yelling at him. "The whole story. Don't leave anything out."

"You know the whole story. Your parents were going out for the evening. They left you with Sonja and me to watch you that night. Something happened—"

"Were they fighting?"

"What?"

"Were. They. Fighting?" Tate demanded a second time, over-emphasizing each word. "Mom and Dad—were they arguing, upset, irritated—were they fighting?"

"They weren't when they dropped you off. Your momma was all smiles as she kissed you goodbye, but who knows what goes on in someone else's relationship?"

"Did my dad ever indicate there was a problem?"

"Your dad had been distracted. Was having trouble winning cases that should have been a lock. That's why I suggested they go out that night." Images of John sitting at his desk that morning flooded his mind. Lee shook the memory and leaned toward Tate. "Look the only ones who know about their marriage were in that car that night when there was a single car accident." Lee hesitated, the decades-old heartache still fresh in his memories. His eyes met Tate's and Lee could see his two-year-old face behind the man in front of him now. The images twisted as much as his stomach twisted inside him.

"Lee?" Tate strained to speak softer. "What are you not telling me?"

"Son, all I know is Belmont ran into them at the restaurant; they had some drinks together, and then he left with them." With each word, Lee wanted to vomit. His reaction to the story had never been as strong as right now. He didn't want to taint the boy's memories of his mother, yet the boy was demanding information.

"Your momma was driving and shouldn't have been. She missed a turn, and the car hit a tree." Even as the words fell from his lips, Lee wondered if he had blamed Carleigh more than he had ever admitted.

"Belmont came to first and pulled Carleigh from the car. She wasn't buckled, so we don't know if she was even alive at that point. Before he could get back for your dad, the car exploded. He was fully engulfed in the flames since he was in the back seat, closest to the gas tank. When the firefighters arrived, they pronounced your momma dead at the scene. Belmont was the only way we knew it was John in the backseat."

"So no DNA testing or fingerprinting or anything on that order was done?"

"Boy, this was more than twenty-five years ago, in the middle of the Mount Pleasant riots, and those tests were expensive. They determined there was a bad gasket leaking and some frayed wiring that sparked the gas fumes. Instant fireball and no one survived. Since Belmont identified the body as John, we had no cause to do any of that."

"We do now."

"You are making absolutely no sense. What is wrong with you?"

"I just went to interview Jack Beacher . . ."

Lee sat forward, interrupting Tate, "I knew that was a bad idea."

Tate slammed his fists down on Lee's desk and leaned toward him, his voice tight as he struggled to keep control. "I don't know who Jack Beacher is, but that man sitting in the interrogation room is *not* him."

Lee shot back, "I swear Tate William Palmer, if you don't stop sounding like a fool and start telling me what's going on—"

Tate threw his arm in the direction of the interrogation room. "That man in there is John William Palmer!" Tate was nearly yelling again as the color suddenly drained from Lee's face.

"*What?* What did you say?" He sank back into his chair.

"I don't know who was in the car with Mom and Belmont that night, but it wasn't Dad. That man sitting down the hall claiming to be Jack Beacher is John Palmer." Tate hesitated, trying to settle himself, focusing on his breathing, and allowed his words to sink in. "My father, your brother, is not dead. So I'm going to ask you again . . . What was going on in their lives?"

Chapter 16

Washington, DC, 1991

With Tate successfully tucked into his aunt's arms, John and Carleigh climbed back into the 1986 Honda Accord. Sitting behind the wheel, John moved the gearshift into reverse, and the tires began to roll backward. Carleigh reached out and switched on the radio, filling the car with happy, bright, melodic sounds of children's voices singing about buses, wheels, and the direction they were going. John let out an audible groan as he put the car in first and pushed the gas. "Please, no."

"I'm not leaving it there, silly." Carleigh grinned as she moved to punch the FM button. As if on cue, George Michael and Aretha Franklin bubbled their way through the speakers. Carleigh giggled and turned the volume up, relishing in the memories that filled her body as she began to sing with the music.

John shifted the car from second into third, reveling in the sound of his wife's joy, and when George met Aretha in a full chorus, John joined Carleigh. His heart soared a little higher when she reached out and placed her hand in his.

As the music faded and some newer, mistimed guitar riffs filled the speakers, Carleigh turned the radio back down. "I'm waiting for you, John."

"Waiting? I'm right here, babe."

"Today, right now, maybe. But you've been battling lately." John could only sigh. Carleigh smiled and squeezed his hand a little tighter, "It's okay, sweetheart, so long as you come back to me. So long as you keep the faith, I'm waiting for you. Deal?"

"Deal," he grinned. He maneuvered the car around Dupont Circle on Massachusetts Avenue and down the much narrower 18th Street toward the small shops, cafés, and restaurants. As he pulled the car into a parking space, he caught a familiar face sitting in the nearest café patio. Before he considered her reaction, John heard the words fall from his mouth, "Uh. I think that's Belmont."

Carleigh's head snapped around. "Where?" Once she confirmed John's initial guess, she turned back to the front of the car and sank into her seat. "You are correct," she muttered. "Why does he have to be here?"

"Well, his office isn't too far from here. Looks like he's with Devin and Henry. They probably had some meeting or something here."

"We don't have to talk to them, do we?"

John studied his wife for a moment. "Well, Belmont is family. If he sees us, I don't think we can just ignore him."

Washington, DC, 2018

"When your history comes to back to bite you, the sting is bad." Jack looked at Millie, and she thought he looked more haggard than she had ever seen him before.

"What do you mean, Jack?" Millie was still trying to make sense of Tate's entrance, reaction, and sudden departure.

"I made a promise I failed to keep." Jack absently picked at his thumb.

Millie watched the man's face. It was almost as if the lines of pain etched themselves there as he spoke. She hesitated, not sure she really wanted any more answers today. Each answer seemed to bring with it more questions. Her chest rose slowly as she drew in a deep breath. "What promise, Jack?"

He rested his head on the table for a few moments. Millie couldn't tell for sure what he was doing, but when Jack lifted his head, she could see the remnants of tears on his cheeks. "I promised Leigh I'd keep the faith. Told her I knew she was waiting for me. I failed to keep that promise."

"Jack . . ."

"As I've said before I've done lots of things I'm not very proud of. Making child porn, kidnapping, selling kids in seedy hotels and on dark roadsides, drug running. But after not keeping the promise to Leigh, probably the biggest regret I have is that of abandoning a two-year-old little boy and not watching him grow into a man."

"Then why not make an effort to visit him?"

"Well, partly because I physically couldn't go, partly because I knew it would be serious trouble, and because he was better off without me, mostly."

"Oh, I'm sure that little boy was not better off without you. You are his father, and little boys need their fathers."

"I think the man who raised him was a better man than I could ever be."

"I agree you have made some terrible choices in your life, but you are still made in the image of God and are worthy of seeing your son grow up to be a man. Do you know where he is now?"

Jack's head hung low enough to almost rest on the table. His words were so soft Millie almost couldn't hear him. "I didn't know until just a few minutes ago." Jack pulled his head higher and looked Millie in the eyes. "But when he opened that door, I knew as soon as I saw him. He looks so much like my dad."

Millie studied Jack's face as he spoke. "Here? Today? The only one I've seen young enough was . . . you mean Tate? Tate Palmer is your son?"

"Yes, ma'am. Tate is my son."

The door to the room suddenly flew open, and Lee charged in. He stared at the man before him as the door slammed shut behind him. His heart raced so hard inside his chest that he couldn't hear anything but its pounding and the rush of blood through his ears. The storm of emotions raged so forcefully, he felt foggy-headed and unsteady. How was he supposed to face the brother he buried over twenty-five years ago?

"I—I couldn't believe Tate. I didn't want to believe that my flesh and blood . . . and yet, here you sit."

"I'm sorry, young man; you are?" Millie, still wrestling with the newest information, adjusted to Lee's presence. "I seem to be having a hard time keeping up with who all the players are today."

Lee's head whipped around to face the other side of the table. "I'm—I'm . . ." he stuttered, "I'm sorry, ma'am." Shallow breaths lead to a deep one as he wrestled for control of his mind, body, and thoughts. "I didn't realize anyone else was in the room." He looked at his brother, as if making sure he was really there, then back to Millie. "Lee," his voice was barely audible. "Lee Palmer." He slowed his mind enough to realize she was not an officer or court clerk he knew. "And your name is?"

She studied his face; it was her heart's turn to race. "Lord," she silently prayed, "what are you doing?" However, all she said out loud was, "Millie Jensen." Lee's eyes grew with recognition.

"Jensen? As in Tana?"

"Yes, Montana is my daughter." She studied Lee for a bit then stood and added, "I think you two boys might need some time alone. Please excuse me, gentlemen." She departed the room and disappeared as the door clicked shut behind her, leaving Lee and John in a confused, disconcerted silence.

Los Angeles, 2017

"So what you are telling me is we have nothing. No one will help my son?" The anger burned inside Silvia's gut.

"I am not telling you that." Chuck knew that was how it sounded. If he was honest with himself, he probably believed that too. An audible sigh slipped from his lips, his shoulders dropping. "Let's face the facts. Hollywood doesn't have anything in place to protect anyone, and children are way down on that list." Still, Chuck wanted, maybe even needed, to give Silvia some hope. There had to be some justice for Greg to be had. "There are others out there. Wade pretty much said everyone has had some kind of experience like this. We just have to find someone else willing to talk about it."

"If someone as big as Wade doesn't want to talk, what is the chance of getting anyone to talk about it?"

"Maybe I need to call Tate back and see if he has any ideas."

"I have a sister . . ." Silvia started, letting her voice trail off as she thought more than spoke.

"What are you thinking?"

"Well, she was actually my sister-in-law, and I haven't seen her since her brother died, but she lives in Maryland. I know Greg needs to go to the event, but maybe he doesn't have to go alone. Maybe I could fly with the group to DC under the guise of a visit, find a way to keep him with me longer, and your friends could watch Greg when I can't?"

"Let me run it past Tate."

Washington, DC, 2018

If staring at a phone would make it ring, Tate would be the master of making people call him. However, the idea of picking up the phone to call Tana and tell her it was his father who destroyed her life all those years ago—he was going to be sick. How does one go about telling someone the man who put them through all of that trauma might one day be their father-in-law—if she would even consider marrying him now, after this. He wasn't sure he would marry him in her situation.

He lay his forehead on his desk, trying to will his mind to slow down. Willing it to clear a little. Searching for a coherent train of thought.

The knock on the door startled him, and he jerked his head up to see her face as the words tumbled from her mouth. "Hi! I just finished across the street and wondered . . ." Tana's eyes caught the crazed look on his face. Her ability to process seemed to be broken—or at least very slow. Were those tears on his face? "What's going on?"

"I think I'm going to be sick."

"Ugh. Are you coming down with the flu?" She walked closer to him, and he instinctively recoiled from her advancement. "Whoa. What—" She froze at the edge of his desk. "What's going on, Tate? You are scaring me."

His voice was thick and cumbersome. "Frankly, I'm scared."

"Of me?"

"Well . . ." He took a deep breath, trying to relax. "Not technically. We, um, we need to have a conversation." He allowed his eyes to meet hers, searching desperately to find the comfort he usually found so readily in them. "I am not very sure how you will react."

Seeing the confusion in her eyes made him drop his own. Feeling the shame of his new reality wash over him anew, he took another deep breath. "And that uncertainty scares me. I am not even sure how I'm reacting, honestly. And that scares me."

"I don't even know what you are saying to me. What is going on?" Before he could answer any further, there was a light knock at the open door, and another woman stepped into the room. Tate looked up and met her eyes. Relief washed over him like an ocean wave.

"Tate, I was worried about you. Baby girl, I'm so glad you are here too."

Tana jerked her head around at the sound of her mother's voice.

"Mom?" She hugged the older woman, nervously laughing, "I am confused. Glad to see you but so confused."

"I'm sure you are. Today is full of surprises."

Tana looked from her mom to Tate and back again. "What are you talking about, Mom? Will someone please tell me what is going on?"

"I have not been able to tell her anything yet, Millie," Tate answered, the weight of the looming conversation full on his shoulders, piercing his heart. Millie stepped in, shutting the door behind her and took the lead.

"Montana, please, sit down. Tate and I have some new information we need to share with you." Tana studied her mom's face. "Please. Sit."

Tana sat across from Tate as her mom began to speak.

"You remember Jack, the man I have been visiting in prison?"

"Of course." She tried to keep the disdain she still wrestled with out of her tone.

"Montana, he has decided to come forth with some new information and asked to have a conversation with Mr. Palmer. Having never talked to Jack before, Mr. Palmer gave the case to Tate and asked him to speak to Jack."

"That much I am aware of, Mom."

179

"Yes, but what we have since learned is that Jack Beacher has not been honest about who he is. Apparently, for a very long time, he has been living under a false identity."

Tate jumped into the conversation, his eyes down, afraid to look Tana in the face for the first time in their relationship. "Tana, what your Mom is trying to tell you is that Jack Beacher's real name is John Palmer." He paused, absently playing with a pen sitting on his desk. Then he looked up and allowed his eyes to meet hers, though he could not bring his voice up much higher than a whisper. "He's my father, Tana."

The revelation left Tana stunned. She looked at Tate with wide eyes. Suddenly the world around her became hazy and slow-moving. "I—I think I need some fresh air." She stood, and Tate and her Mom also stood. She waved them off. "No. Don't. I'll call you. I just need to go right now." And she left the room. Tate started after her.

"Tate," Millie said softly. "It's better to let her clear her head." He turned to face her, his eyes wide with fear. "I know it's hard, son. However, she will come around faster if you let her have some time." He sank into his chair, looking lost and alone. Millie knelt beside him. "I don't know where you are with Jesus, but can I pray with you?

"Pray? What does prayer do now? She's gone."

Millie smiled. Tate half-wondered if she was crazy. Or maybe sadistic. When he realized she was talking, he shook the thought from his mind.

"Oh, she's not gone. I know this feels impossible. I know that weight sitting on your chest right this minute. But there is good news, Tate."

"Good news? How can anything good be found in this?"

"I can't answer that. I can tell you Jesus told a crowd of rulers surrounding Him, what is impossible with man is possible with God."

Tate dropped his eyes back to the ground. "I don't even know what that means."

"What that means, son, is that God takes situations that feel hopeless to man, things meant to destroy man, and turns them into blessings so large that they are not containable."

Slowly, Tate's eyes lifted to meet Millie's again. "How is it possible to turn a kidnapping and death—fake death—into anything positive?"

She let his words settle in the room. "I'll be completely honest with you, Tate. I don't know. I didn't know the day Montana disappeared from my life. I didn't know every day for eight years. I didn't know every time I walked into the prison where Jack has done time for his crime. And yet, one day, when my hope was the lowest it had ever been, an agent walked into my living room and told me they found my daughter." She paused, gathering her thoughts as the idea sunk in. "God is the God of the impossible. I don't know how. I don't know His plans. I do know He is good. Even when it feels impossible, He is good."

"How can you say that?"

"Because I've watched goodness bloom out of impossible. That's what God does for those who love Him."

Tate shook his head. "I don't understand."

Sighing, Millie confessed, "I don't understand either. I just know it happens. I've seen it with these old eyes." Once more, she found her smile, "The beautiful thing is, Tate, you don't have to understand. You only have to choose to trust. Jesus paid for it; whether you choose to or not, it's paid for. It's a gift sitting in front of you. You choose to pick it up or walk away. That is the choice you have right now. Take the gift He's given and trust Him to work it out, or you stay in a prison of anger and bitterness."

"I don't know how to make that choice. There is so much anger inside me right now."

"I understand. That anger is a crushing weight on your chest. And you can hold onto it. Or you can ask Jesus to be the Lord and Savior of your life, give Him the anger, and choose to trust Him."

Chapter 17

Washington, DC, 2018

"I know you are going to need way more explanation than I can honestly give." John watched his brother pace in front of the two-way mirror after Millie left them alone. "Truth is, I am hazy on that night. I remember going for dinner and having a rather tense conversation. I thought she had been cheating on me."

"Carleigh?" Lee growled. "That is the most ridiculous thing I've ever heard. That woman loved you more than I have ever seen anyone love another human being." He turned to face his brother. Lee couldn't tell if he was angry with his brother or saddened by all the time lost over the years, but he knew frustration was exploding in his chest. "Why didn't you talk to me?"

"I was trying to find out on my own. I was following Leigh to a house, not very far from yours, actually. She would go early every Thursday morning." John's mind drifted back to that last chilly morning. "She would go in and about an hour, maybe ninety minutes later, she would come back out. Like clockwork. So I confronted her that night. After drinking several drinks, I honestly cannot remember what she said, or even leaving the restaurant. I vaguely remember Belmont pulling me from the car, but it was the next day when he told me what I did—and what needed to happen."

"What you did?" Lee was trying to keep up with the new information. The conversation with Tate played over in his mind, and John's words began to sink in. "Wait. Belmont knew you were alive?" The shock was almost more than he could bear. He sat down in the chair Millie once occupied. "He—he helped with all the arrangements." Lee's anger grew as reality became apparent. "He lied to my face. And has continued to lie to my face every time I have seen him." He let this truth tumble in his head. Something John said clicked in Lee's mind. "The house was close to mine. On Thursdays?"

"Yes."

Lee winced in disgust at John's admission. "Ugh. John. I wish you had talked to me. Why do you have to be so stubborn?" John just stared at him. "There was no affair. It was a Bible study, John. Carleigh and Sonja were attending a Bible study together."

"What are you talking about? I never once saw Sonja, or anyone else for that matter, there."

"Our house was on the back side of that one, and Sonja used to walk through the alley and in the back door when she would go. . . . Sonja invited me, but I didn't want to go. Not until after . . ." He stopped short his explanation. His thought train jumped the track again. "Belmont knew? This whole time? How did he know where to find you?"

"Leigh once called him a viper. I had no idea how right she was until this event. Like I said, hazy on the details. But that night turned my world upside down too.

"I never learned how it was he was there that night. I honestly didn't want to know how or why he showed up at the restaurant. I kind of remember him there at dinner. Later, Belmont said I had been driving drunk. I hit the tree, and the crash killed Carleigh.

"So he moved her to look like she was driving, put a homeless man's body in place of mine, and burned the whole thing. He said he saved me from murder charges. Told me I killed her and would have gone to jail for it.

"So between the money I owed him and the murder of my wife, I had nothing left. I have lived under his control and corruption every day since. When I got arrested six years later, I told him I didn't want to fight the charges. I belonged here anyway." John caught his brother's gaze and held it. "I am done covering for him. Whatever the consequences I may face, I don't care. And that . . . that is why I am here now."

Washington, DC, 2017

Landing in a plane always made Silvia's stomach a little queasy. This time, her stomach threatened to explode all over the seat in front of her. Or maybe it wasn't the landing. Maybe it was the fact they were landing in DC or that she had to let her son out of her sight, under the protection of Stan—if one could call his watch protection at all. That was like asking a fox to protect baby chicks. The party was only one night, but it meant Greg staying with Stan while she drove to Maryland. Without letting Stan and his father know they were watching them, they couldn't come up with anything else.

"Hey, Mom?" Greg's voice was a welcome intrusion into her own.

"Yes, baby?" she smiled at the boy. "Can you stay in DC for a little longer and take me sightseeing?"

Silvia paused, her thoughts traveling ahead of her in time. She had about eight years left with him before he would be an adult and on his own. And a few less before he wanted nothing more than to hang out with friends as a teenager. She didn't want this period to slip by in a blur of time not spent with Greg. She found a smile for him. "I would love to. Let's look at that schedule Stan gave you. We might be able to work some things into it."

Washington, DC, 2018

Tana found herself walking toward West Potomac Park. Being in the area of the memorials that stood for so much freedom and fighting for the things of life that matter was always a comfort to her soul. She wandered down the trail of the Vietnam Veterans Memorial. She was always fascinated by the growing quiet as one walked toward the middle of the memorial, and she was desperate for quiet. She slowed her walk and pretended to read names from the memorial. Though the physical quiet was a comfort, it wasn't helping quiet the questions in the depth of her soul. And the presence of the tourists was not helping either, so she kept walking.

How was she to face this reality? How could a God who loved her allow her to fall in love with the son of her tormentor? Okay, so Jack, or John, or whoever he was—he wasn't the actual perpetrator of torment but more guilty by association. He delivered her into the hands of her tormentor. How was this an acceptable event for her to have to deal with now?

Tana felt as if each step cleared a little more fog. Long walks and fresh air helped her slow her breathing and gave her space to corral her thoughts. She continued to wander past the Lincoln Memorial and eventually into the park. She allowed her mind to shuffle thoughts here and then and ponder all that was currently in front of her. As if she could pull them out of the tumbling dryer one at a time, examine them, and place them in the pile where they belonged. Some to be lightly considered and some to be fully contemplated.

She landed on the fact, no matter what was going on around her, she had completely fallen in love with Tate. He had proved himself to be amazing and wonderful and a safe place. And this was going to be a trial, but it would not change who Tate was—the incredible, genuine heart of him as a man.

This man, Jack, was Tate's father the day he kidnapped her, and Tate was still the amazing man he was yesterday. What was it Kay had said to her? It was time to learn the mercy of forgiveness. Maybe it was time to learn another aspect of that forgiveness. She was forgiven, so maybe it was time to do the forgiving.

Washington, DC, 2017

Parties, no matter what city, felt the same to Greg. They were loud, overpowering, and uncomfortable. Walking the red carpet was nerve-racking, with people crowding around, cameras flashing, and others sticking microphones in your face, asking lots of crazy questions.

Yet Greg smiled and waved as he walked, mostly doing his best to copy Wade Bale's actions. He knew if he did as Wade did, he would be fine. Walking as close to them as Stan would allow—follow but not too closely, were his instructions—Greg waved to the crowd and talked to the same reporters the others talked to.

Scattered throughout the building, security guards kept a watchful eye over the proceedings. And waiting inside the party were the "who's who" of DC senators, lawyers, wealthy socialites, and important business men, all mingling with the actors and other LA connections. Tana stood watching the large "who's who" list of DC and LA people hobnob, totally unaware of the searching going on in the offices nearby. This was the last place Tana expected to find herself while working a case. And yet, here she was.

She turned to her left and watched as Tate made his way, drinks in hand, toward her. Here was an incredibly handsome man. So many things in that thought just astounded her.

Once more facing the front of the room, she watched as Greg made his way in, cameras still flashing from the press held outside. "Do you know for sure which one is Stan?" Tate asked.

She looked from Greg to Tate, now standing beside her, and back again. "Honestly, I'm not sure from this distance."

"Well." Tate handed her a glass of ginger ale. "Let's find out, shall we?"

Washington, DC, 2018

Lee and Tate sat across the desk from one another in what would appear to an unknowing onlooker to be peaceful tranquility. An unwinding of a Friday night, preparation for the weekend. Except it was only 3:30 in the afternoon. Neither mouth moved, their bodies sat limp in their chairs. But upon closer observation, their eyes were in far-off dances of remembrance. The events of the afternoon, the conversations and explanations, ricocheted in their minds like pinballs.

"I'm so sorry to have put you through all of this, son. I should have picked someone else to talk to him first."

Tate, a bit startled by the noise, rebutted his uncle's concern. "And delay the reality? No. This is the best way for it to have gone. Besides, anyone else walking into that room would have seen Jack Beacher and only Jack Beacher."

"If you want out—"

"Of course I want out. I want to be two and wake up in my own room, with Momma cooking breakfast, none of this have ever happened. But that cannot be. As far as the case is concerned, I think we need to go federal. I don't think any of us should do anything more than be witnesses on the stand—anything else could get it thrown out."

"You have a suggestion?"

"Yeah, actually, I do." Tate stood to his feet. "However, I need to run my thoughts by Tana first. Can we continue this in the morning? Maybe have everyone meet at the house?"

"Absolutely." He watched his nephew stand up and turn to leave. Lee could still see that sweet two-year-old in this grown man. "Hey, boy . . ." Tate stopped in his tracks and slowly turned back to face his uncle. "I just want to make sure you know I love you and am very proud of the man you are."

Tate smiled slightly, probably for the first time that day. "Thank you, sir. I love you too."

As Tate walked out of his office for the second time that afternoon, Lee picked up the handset of his desktop phone. His hands were shaking enough to make dialing difficult. His mouth was dry; his tongue felt thick and inflexible. Immovable. His mind raced. How would he even begin to tell Sonja that John was alive? Or that there was a story she needed to hear, knowing full well she would not want this information.

"Hello?" As soon as he heard her voice, Lee knew he could not tell her over the phone. She and Carleigh had been close. Had been even before the boys met them. Best friends. When Carleigh died, so did part of Sonja's heart. No. He had to tell her in person.

"Hey, sweetheart." His voice was low to keep it from cracking.

"Ooooh, you don't sound good. What's going on?" He laughed. Her insight was strong; always had been.

"We need to talk. Now. I know it's early, but can you meet me?"

"Absolutely. Where?"

Lee didn't have to think long. He knew his wife. Sensitive. Private. Loving. Not long after the police informed them of John and Carleigh's deaths, she got rid of the couch, as it was a constant reminder of that conversation. "How soon can you get home?"

"Probably twenty minutes."

"Fabulous. Let's meet on the swings." They had decided shortly after, if they had to have a tough conversation or if they were fighting about something, they would go out to the swings. They held hands and let the motion of the swings settle their spirits.

Sonja laughed lightly. "That bad, huh?"

"Oh, yeah. That bad." Lee took a deep breath. He could almost hear her contemplating his answer, but before she could respond, he said, "I love you, Sonja," and hung up the phone.

The breeze coming off the Potomac was the most soothing thing she had felt all day. All at once, Tana knew she needed to talk to Tate. She lifted her head, wiped the tears from her eyes, and squared her shoulders. Reaching into her pocket, Tana pulled out her phone and sent him a quick text, asking if he could meet her. Since he had just left his uncle's office, he told her he would be there in just a few minutes, and she assured him she would wait.

Upon his arrival, Tana stood and embraced him. Shock rippled through his body at the greeting he did not expect, it took him a moment to wrap his arms around her. As he allowed himself to believe she was hugging him, he relaxed into the embrace, and they stood together for several minutes. When Tana began to let go, she stepped back and looked Tate in the eyes. "I cannot begin to understand the emotions you are holding. I am going to ask that someday, when you are ready, if we can talk about them. For now," she reached out and took his hands, "I need you to know this one thing only, and that nothing else beyond this matters. I love you, Tate Palmer." Tate caught his breath and started to object. "No. Nothing else matters. I don't care. My next step is to talk to Mom."

"Your mom?"

"She is the strongest person I have ever known, and I need to find some strength."

"There is going to be so much to talk about."

"I know. Until I talk with her, I don't know that I can consider anything else."

"Okay. Let's talk to your mom. Then," he took her hands in his, "I think we need to call your uncles. But first, I want to talk about my conversation with your mom after you left the room."

"Ha. I kind of forgot she was even there; my mind was in such a fog."

"Mine too," Tate agreed. "That conversation helped bring some clarity to my mind. And as I prayed with her, I asked Jesus to forgive my hatred of my father . . . and be my savior."

Tana's heart leaped inside her chest. "Oh, Tate!" She threw her arms around him again, and a second time, Tate was stunned by her reaction. Tana continued speaking her thoughts. "I am so excited for you. I bet Mom was thrilled."

Chapter 18

Washington, DC, 2018

"We need a game plan." Lee paced the living room floor. "Bringing down someone like Belmont is not going to be an easy road." He stopped directly across the coffee table from Tate and sat on the sofa. "He has connections." Sonja walked into the room with three cups of hot coffee.

"I have an idea." He took a cup from his aunt. "Thank you, Nini." Looking back at his uncle, he said, "I talked it over with Tana, and she agrees it's a good one."

Sonja handed her husband the second cup and sat beside him. "Okay, let me hear it."

"First, we need some help. Tana is making that call today. As soon as she gets her answer, she'll come over." He hesitated just a bit. "Look, I know the timing is off, so I am not sure about when yet, but can I get your opinion on something?" He reached into his pocket and pulled out a box.

Sonja gasped, her hands covering her mouth. "Oh Tate! Is that what I think it is?"

"Well, if you think it's a diamond ring . . ." He opened the box and handed it to her, and continued, "you might be right. I love her, Nini. I want to spend the rest of my life with her."

Sonja jumped up and hugged the young man.

"I am so excited for you, son. And very proud." Lee wrapped his arms around them both.

Washington, DC, 2017

Their movement through the crowd was not easy. Tana marveled at just how packed the hotel could be. "How many people are here?"

"The security detail was given a guest list of five hundred," Tate scanned the crowd before he faced her to speak. "I'm going to guess we are actually pushing the seven-hundred-limit."

"What is it about this movie that warrants such a crowd?"

"I think it's a combination of the movie and the political side. Since Senator West is here, he will use the opportunity to campaign as much as he can."

"Hey, buddy."

The voice stopped Tate in his tracks. He spun around to delight. "Chuck Blue!" He stepped toward the man, extending his hand. "Man, it's been much too long. You have to stop hiding in LA!"

"I'm here now, aren't I?" Their handshake slid into a bear hug as the two men laughed. "It's so good to see you, Tate. I don't think you have changed much in the last five years."

"I may not have, but what is with this hair?" Tate playfully flipped a lock off Chuck's shoulder.

"LA, man. You have to keep up with the hip styles if you want to appear with it enough to photograph the top stars."

Tate shook his head, his grin stretching from ear to ear. Turning toward Tana, he offered formal introductions. "Chuck, this is my girlfriend, Montana Jensen. Tana, this is Chuck Blue, photographer to the stars and one of my best college buddies."

Reaching out to capture his hand, Tana smiled. "It's so nice to meet you, Chuck. College buddies, huh? I think we need a long walk down memory lane. I'm sure you have some fantastic stories I need to hear."

Chuck returned her grin. "Oh, for sure."

"Chuck!" A new voice, deep and oddly familiar, came from behind Tana. She turned to see a face she knew, though she wasn't sure where they had met.

"Hey! It's good to see you, Wade. Can I introduce you to my friends? This is Tate Palmer and Montana Jensen. Tate and Tana, this is *the* Wade Bale, top actor in LA."

"It's nice to meet you, Tate and Montana."

"Please, my friends call me Tana."

"Tana. Mine call me Mr. Bale, sir." He paused for a second, judging reactions.

Chuck cracked first. "Wade."

Wade cracked a smile. "Or Wade. That usually goes over better outside of a movie studio." The others chuckled at him. "How do the two of you know Chuck?"

"Chuck was a senior my freshman year of college," Tate offered.

"Yeah, one year of living in a suite with me was all the kid could take."

Shaking Wade's hand Tate offered, "Thank you for your phone call. Between your testimony and Greg's, I am sure the search will pay off."

"Shhh. Not so loud. Everyone here has ears."

"Hey, Mr. Wade!" The four adults turned to see Greg and the entourage headed their way.

Grateful for the topic change, Wade answered, "Greg! How was sightseeing with your mom today?"

"It was so cool! Did you know there are massive amounts of tunnels under this city?"

"Oh, yeah?"

"Yeah! Like nine to ten feet tall. Some of them are so big, a person could drive an SUV through them! Mr. Stan told me he could take me through a few since his dad is a senator."

As if on cue, the man walked out of the crowd. "Hey, Greg, there you are." He turned to see those who were chatting with Greg. "Hi! I'm Stan West." He extended a hand to Tate and then Tana.

"Tate Palmer, DC lawyer. My girlfriend, Tana Jensen."

Washington, DC, 2018

Their Saturday morning routine was a quiet time for them to catch up with each other. To shut out the craziness of their day-to-day. A time to pretend the ugly, seedy part of their lives was non-existent. It had taken them years of crazy schedules to both finally be on mostly nine to five, five days a week work life. Not that Paul was thrilled with being behind a desk, but he did like having consistent time with his wife.

Michelle and Paul sat at the table on their porch, enjoying the warmth of the Virginia sun and a cup of coffee. On days like these, Paul's mind would wander a bit too much. There were two days in his career Paul often thought about when he slowed down. And they were connected to the same case. The little girl lost and found.

Usually, the finding finished the case. Somehow, this one never really felt finished. Oh, it looked good on paper, but Paul was pretty sure there was more to it. There was something he was missing. Like it was too easy. And it bugged him. She was found and returned home, the abductor arrested, and yet, that guy didn't feel right. He didn't feel capable enough or driven enough or edgy enough or—or what? Paul would try to shake it from his mind, but he couldn't put his finger on it. It kept coming back to him. It felt more like a Band-aid and less like healing.

Paul pretended to skim the newspaper, and Michelle turned the pages of a travel magazine as their pups, two papillons named Shaggy and Scooby, rested nearby when Paul's phone interrupted their tranquility.

"Don't they know it's Saturday?" Michelle gently teased her husband. "You don't do Saturday anymore."

Reaching for the device, Paul quipped, "I'll remind them with a strong lashing."

Turning the phone to face himself, a hardly noticeable *Huh* escaped his lips, just enough for Michelle to glance up and study his face. Work? Personal? She couldn't read his expression, and that wasn't normal. "Montana, what a pleasant surprise," Paul spoke into the phone.

Montana. No wonder she couldn't read his face. That sweet child was usually pretty predictable—birthdays, anniversaries, holidays. Out of the blue was not her style.

Michelle picked up her coffee cup without removing her eyes from her husband's face. The man could play poker with the best of them with his stony affect. When he didn't want his emotions to show, you did not see them. Except in his eyes. He still had trouble with his eyes giving him away when he was upset. Then, and only then, could you see the fire burning deep inside them. Michelle began to see the flames flicker.

She raised the cup to her lips before she realized it was empty. This phone call, whatever it was, was probably going to demand another cup. She started to stand when Paul reached out and grabbed her hand. That second cup was going to have to wait.

"I understand, honey. Yes, Mitch and I will meet you there in an hour. You did the right thing. Have you called Troy yet? Yep. Perfect. See you soon."

Standing at the table, her hand in his, Michelle waited for him to end the call. When he set the phone down, she said, "I'll get dressed."

College Park, Maryland, 2018

After a day like today, Henry West needed a stiff drink. He flipped the light on as he made his way into the study. This was his favorite room in the whole house. He loved the cherry hardwood floors, trim, and backlit bookshelves. The leather sitting chairs faced the fireplace, and arched windows overlooked their modest, twenty-five-acre wooded lot. There wasn't anything Henry didn't love about the room, including the small wet bar alcove in the bookshelves.

Quickly, Henry moved from the doorway to the marble-topped shelf and pulled a Glencairn glass from the cabinet. He started to admire once again the etched *W*, only to be distracted by the slight shaking in his hands. The glasses were a gift from Belmont, and he didn't want to break them. Maybe several drinks were in order. He lifted the tongs to grab a chunk of ice from the bucket on the counter. It slipped from his grasp.

Definitely, several drinks were in order.

He picked the ice up again, managed to place it in the glass, allowing it to cool the auburn liquid as it slid over the frozen ball. Henry lifted his glass and inhaled the sweet caramel and honeysuckle aroma. This fiftieth anniversary of the small-batch was his perfect pour. Henry sipped the liquid slowly, swirling it around his mouth before swallowing. He enjoyed the fig, peach, and oak mixture.

Indeed, a luxurious treat.

However, at over two thousand dollars a bottle, he wasn't getting loaded on it. He set the bottle back and grabbed the straight bourbon whiskey bottle. It was much easier to get drunk spending thirty dollars. And he still enjoyed the fruity, floral taste.

After he finally swallowed, Henry, along with the bottle, moved to his executive desk. The more traditional and grand desk, made of cherry and mahogany woods, made Henry feel powerful, masculine, and important—untouchable, even. He took a deep breath, picked up the bottle, and poured another drink. Finally, Henry sat back in his chair, placing his feet on the corner of the desk.

It's my job to root out the bad guys and find the children, to pull them out of horrible situations.

Tana's words rung loud in his ears. Just who did she think she was, this Montana Jensen? Who was she to determine what defined a horrible situation? Those kids should be grateful for his time and attention! Henry could tell you just who she was: an immense pain in the . . .

"Drinking a little, are we?"

Henry nearly spilled the whole bottle of bourbon. "Sh-Sh-Shire!" His feet hit the floor as he hollered at the shadowy figure standing in the doorway. "Come in and shut the door. My wife will see you."

"Your wife?" Devin repeated as he stepped into the room, shutting the door shut behind him. "Did you forget she went to her sister's cabin this morning?" As he watched the man fumbling to clean his mess, Devin could only wonder why Belmont had orchestrated Henry West, as incompetent as he was, to become the senator from New Hampshire.

Henry knocked out a third shot. "Oh, crap. You're right. I totally forgot. No wonder it's so quiet here." He let out a soft giggle. "That woman can run her mouth! Come. Sit. Would you like a drink?" Henry removed the wire-framed glasses from his face and rubbed his eyes before returning them to sit on his nose.

"No. Thank you."

"Seriously, I've never known you to turn down a good bourbon." Shire just shrugged his shoulders, still standing behind the chairs at Henry's desk.

"How did the deposition go today?" Devin ran a finger along the top wood finish of the chair to his left, his eyes never leaving Henry as he waited for an answer.

"Eh. What can I tell you? I didn't say much. Derby did most of the talking." Henry downed another shot before he actually looked at Devin—if you could call it that. His eyes were feeling a little blurry. "Man, sit down. You're making me nervous."

Shire didn't move toward a seat in front of Henry. Instead, he moved toward the edge of the desk and leaned on it. "You still got that pistol we talked about last month?"

"The Colt? Of course. Why would I get rid of it?"

"I wanna see it. Is it handy?"

"Man, it's locked in a gun safe. One has to be careful these days."

"Of course. I still want to see it. You know I am a history buff."

Henry raised an eyebrow as if that gave him a clearer insight into Devin's thoughts. Then he leaned forward and pulled a drawer from its resting place. Inside was a little gray case, neatly tucked away. He pulled it out and set it on top of the leather topper on his desk. He pulled the pen drawer open and removed a small key from its place. He unlocked the metal case. "There it is. The Colt M1911A1 my dad carried in World War II."

"It's a .45-caliber, right?" Devin didn't wait for a response as he moved the gun from his left hand to his right, looking at both sides of the weapon, taking note of the "United States Property" still clearly legible. "What a nice weapon."

"I know. Dad was pretty proud of that. He actually found this one on the battlefield and pocketed it. He turned in the one he was issued but didn't turn this one in."

"Sneaky."

"I suppose so."

"Must run in the family." Devin looked up at Henry, gauging the reaction to his jab. He got none. Once more, he turned his attention to the dark metal in his hands. Cold steel. Rough grip. Loose trigger. He held his hands out and sighted the barrel. It might be off just a hair. Not too bad for its age. "Do you shoot it often?"

"No. That thing is old. I would be afraid it would jam and maybe even explode. Guns do that, you know." Devin flipped it around again, pointing it toward the ground this time. Henry was getting antsy. "Why are you here, Devin?"

"What? A person can't visit an old friend?"

"A person can. You don't. What gives?"

Devin looked at his friend. He almost felt sorry for the guy. If Devin had feelings, he would have felt sorry for him. Devin shrugged. "Belmont's not exactly thrilled you were being deposed today."

Henry snorted. "Me either. I thought Belmont was better at keeping us out of the sights of the DA."

Now it was Devin's turn to laugh. "Since when is it his problem? You have a job to do, and you let other . . . things . . . get in the way."

"I get my job done, thank you very much." Henry could feel the rage building inside him. Or maybe it was the alcohol speaking; he wasn't sure. "You can tell Belmont to—"

Devin had the barrel up against Henry's temple with a flick of his wrist, cutting his words short. "I don't think Belmont likes how much fear of him you have lost over the years, Henry."

Henry swallowed hard. "I'm done fearing him."

"Yes, you are." Devin tightened his finger hold on the gun until there was a small, metallic click.

Henry sneered. "Do you really think I'm stupid enough to hand you a loaded weapon?"

"Nope. Just testing. The boss wanted you to know how angry he is with you before you die."

"But I know you well enough, and I am not messing around with you."

"Yep." Devin reached behind him and unholstered another pistol. "That's why I brought my own." The muzzle flashed, lighting up the stunned look on Henry's face. "That's the difference between us, old friend." Devin turned, set both weapons on the desk, and began dismantling them. "I stayed prepared, and you got sloppy."

Devin reached into his pocket, producing two latex gloves and a small, dark, microfiber cloth. Quickly he slid his hands inside the gloves. Next, he switched the two barrels, reassembled the two firearms, swapped the two clips, wiping everything down as he worked, before placing his back in his holster. "You would be amazed what you can find on the internet, Henry." He placed Henry's weapon against his head and the trigger finger on the trigger, then let the hand drop and the gun fall to the floor. "Oh, wait. No, you wouldn't be surprised. You're dead." He moved back around the desk and headed for the front door. "Goodbye, Henry."

Chapter 19

Washington, DC, 2017

"I really don't like watching that child walk off with Stan." The pit in Tana's stomach grew with each step Stan and Greg took away from her.

"I know. But we have to catch them in the act or find images on his computer. We can't just say we know what's going on and arrest him," Tate reminded her.

"Just because I understand the process, doesn't mean I have to like it." Tana shifted on her heels.

"You seem fidgety."

"This process is why I choose to work behind my computer."

"I don't like it either."

Tana sighed. "Just how far do we have to let them get ahead of us?"

"Ahead of us? Right now, they have to at least leave the party. I mean, nothing is going to happen to the kid if they stay here."

"Do they know we are watching? They don't really seem to be in any kind of hurry."

"Come on." Tate grabbed her hand and led her straight toward Stan and Greg.

"What are you doing?"

"I'm taking you to the dance floor."

"What?" Her objection was much more vocal than physical as he lead her through the crowd.

Tate pulled her out on the floor and spun around to face her, his arm sliding around the small of her back and gently pulling her body much nearer to his. "Killing two birds with one stone. Maybe even three."

"What are you talking about?"

"This way, we can keep an eye on Greg, without looking like we are keeping an eye on him. And I get to dance with my favorite dance partner."

"And the third?"

"Third, we can move closer to them, without seeming out of place."

Washington, DC, 2018

Paul and Michelle walked into the living room of the Palmer household, led by Tana. Sonja, Lee, and Tate greeted their visitors kindly. More coffee warmed their cups and the introductions buzzed around the room.

As the small talk waned, Lee changed the subject.

"Despite my desire to, I have yet to call my cousin. Partly, because I am not sure how to make that call, and partly because I am afraid if I tell Belmont I know John is alive, he would have him killed in prison."

Paul set his coffee cup down on the table, "It sounds like that's a valid fear. I have had some guys do some digging on him. It looks like he's represented some rather significant trafficking cases. This fact alone would give him strong connections there. If all your brother says is true, I do not doubt he would be able to have him killed with little effort." He leaned forward and added, "We must be careful with how much information we make known. My guess is, even a small hint would set in motion some dangerous actions."

"It is for that reason I have not confronted him."

"I would suggest no one outside of this room become informed until we have Belmont in custody. To the rest of the world, John is simply Jack Beacher. Do you have any idea how close Belmont keeps track of him?"

"If he doesn't know yet, I would guess the fact that he is in DC will get to Belmont quickly. And that alone could be trouble. When Belmont hears, I'm sure he will start asking questions. If he hears Jack has been to our office, I'm sure that will be the end of it."

"So how do we keep him safe while we try to prove Belmont is not as squeaky clean as he likes to pretend?" Tate asked. "I mean to prove all Jack is saying is going to take time. And keeping his location unknown to Belmont will probably, in and of itself, raise questions for Belmont."

"You are probably correct, Tate. So our goal is to be as quiet and low-key with this investigation as we possibly can," Paul agreed. The ring of the phone in the kitchen went mostly unnoticed until a pale Sonja walked back into the room, the receiver in hand.

"Lee." Her tone was quiet and oddly unsteady. "It's Belmont." Every head snapped in her direction and watched as she made her way to Lee.

Taking the phone from her, Lee glanced at Paul. "Hello?" Everyone else held their breath, leaning toward Lee in hopes of hearing the other end of the conversation. They wore their emotions in full view as some chewed thumb nails, some twirled hair, and others watched their cups of coffee as if they were about to do parlor tricks.

Lee pulled the receiver away from his ear and shut it off without saying anything. He turned and squarely faced the waiting group.

"Well, Paul, we no longer need to worry about what Belmont will do when he finds out we are on to him. He is on his way to China."

"What?" Tate exclaimed. "China?"

"Yes." Lee returned to his seat. "They do not have an extradition treaty with us. So even when we can put our case together, we will not be able to touch him."

"That doesn't solve our issue," Paul quietly reminded them as he pulled his phone from his pocket and started searching for numbers.

"Keeping Jack alive?" Lee questioned. "No, it does not."

"I think I need to go see him." The voice was almost a whisper; Lee wasn't sure he heard correctly.

"What?" he stammered a bit, "What did you say?"

Tana looked at Lee. "I want to talk to Jack face to face. Before anything else, before we ever get into a courtroom." She took a breath and looked toward Paul and then Tate. "Mom," she turned to face Millie. "I want to follow your lead.

Washington, DC, 2017

"You know if he gets the boy into the tunnels, there will be trouble, right?" Wade tried to remain as neutral as he could. Yet even he had to admit this needed to stop somewhere.

Tana studied him for a moment. "You have a better idea?"

"Maybe." Wade pulled the two of them off to the side of the room, away from most of the crowd. "What if I can show you the way to the room they will use? Could you do anything then to stop him?"

"That will depend on what all we find there," Tate admitted.

Washington, DC, 2018

"Saturday afternoon at the office. So weird. So quiet." Lee and Sonja walked into the room to find Tate, Tana, and Millie waiting on them.

Paul and Michelle had not yet arrived. They were picking Troy up at the airport. Glancing at his watch, Lee thought that should be soon.

"I don't know, Uncle Lee. I've pulled more than one Saturday afternoon or even Sunday making sure the case files are right for Monday morning." He paused, studying his uncle's face, the etched lines betraying his weariness. Not just in his face, but deeper. His uncle's eyes, if they truly are the window to the soul, revealed the effects of this whole event. "If I were a betting man, I would wager the surrealistic events of the last few days is what you find odd."

Lee smiled. "I am sure that is a wager you would win, young man."

Tana wanted to make sure they were all on the same page. "I know we have much going on. But before we do anything else, Mom, will you please pray for me?" She pulled Tate's hand a little closer to them. "Over us?"

Washington, DC, 2017

"Are you ready to see the tunnels, Greg?"

"Yes, sir," Greg admitted. "But, can Mr. Wade come too? I think he would like to see the tunnels."

Stan and Henry exchanged glances. "Oh, wouldn't that be fun?" Stan answered, before pretending to look around the room. "But I don't see him, and we can't be gone from the party too long. Is that okay?"

Greg sighed. "I guess so."

"Good! Come on!"

Together, Greg, Stan, and Henry moved toward a single door to the back of the room, with a dimly-lit sign that read "stairs." The door swung open easily, and they began their descent. Halfway down the flight of stairs, they met another party: Tana, Tate, and several officers.

"What are you doing?" the senator demanded.

His rant was interrupted by his son, "Hey, how did you get my laptop?"

One of the officers stepped forward. "Senator West, Mr. West, you are both under arrest for possession of child pornography."

Washington, DC, 2018

After spending the night in the local lock-up, John once again found himself in an interrogation room, though he wasn't exactly sure what to expect this afternoon. It's not every Saturday he found himself in the box. Even though he didn't have any idea how things would go when he walked into the office yesterday, today he felt even more disconnected and vulnerable. He had put his life in the hands of the people he had betrayed a quarter of a century before, and he couldn't begin to predict what they would do now.

When the door opened, Millie walked in. Somehow this was a tremendous comfort to him. She was followed by Tate and a young woman he had not seen before. Millie spoke as she walked in, "Good morning, Ja . . ." She hesitated at the sound of the name she had known him by. "I'm sorry—John. That one might take a little getting used to." He nodded in response.

"I guess I don't know what to call you either. Dad doesn't feel right. Neither does John." Tate watched him quizzically.

Picking at his fingernails and trying to steady his breathing, he replied. "Jack is fine. John has been dead for a long time and I, I never earned Dad."

"Okay, Jack. I have a young lady here who has something to say to you." He turned to face the dark-haired beauty. "Montana . . ." Turning back toward Jack, Tate watched the color drain from the older man's face as he realized who the young lady was. Jack turned to face Millie, almost as if he were looking for reassurance from her.

"It's alright, Jack," the older woman offered.

"Hello, Jack. My name is Tana Jensen, and yes, I was that little girl twenty-three years ago. You ripped me from my family and turned my life into a living nightmare." She paused and breathed deeply, trying to find strength, or courage, or just the will to continue. "I—I wanted to take this time to speak directly to you." She lifted her head to look him directly in the eyes. Jack could not face her, so he looked down toward the table.

"Not in front of anyone else, not in a courtroom, just us." Tana took another deep breath. Jack braced himself for what he could only believe would be the onslaught of a verbal lashing. Instead, she moved to his side of the table, knelt beside his chair, and like a mother gently lifting a child's face, looked him directly in the eyes again. "Jack, I forgive you." She took a third deep breath, the sting of tears in her eyes. John felt all the air suddenly sucked from the room. "I forgive you. I know you had evil intentions, but God can do good with it. You made life awful, but God redeemed it. Having been forgiven of my own sins, I now do the same for you. You are forgiven."

Jack, wide-eyed, stumbled over his own words. "Why? How? I don't—You can't . . . I—I don't . . ." and then he stopped as tears began to roll from his eyes.

Chapter 20

Washington, DC, 2018

Sitting on the patio of a local coffee shop, Tana savored the calm of the moment. The warmth of the sun on her cheeks filled Tana with such joy, she didn't care that the light breeze from the Potomac River tossed her hair into her coffee. After tucking the rogue strand behind her ear yet again, she closed her eyes and allowed her shoulders to relax.

Now that the Cherry Blossom Festival was over, the crowd around the area had settled to a dull roar. There were still a few blossoms scattered on the Weeping Cherry trees, enough Tana could still smell their fragrance in the air.

Opening her eyes, Tana reached for her coffee mug, the sunlight glistening off the diamond now on her left hand. The ring and all that had changed over the last few years brought a broader smile to her lips.

Tate spotted Tana and stood looking between her and the trees as he relished the joy and contentment beating in his chest. "Good morning, beautiful," he offered as he moved closer to her table.

"Good morning, charming," she answered without looking behind her.

Taking the seat beside her, he asked, "What is it you like about these trees so much?"

Tana laughed. "You think I need a reason beyond the fact they are so beautiful?"

"All of the cherry trees are pretty. Why are these your favorite?" He set his mug on the table and pulled out his chair.

She pondered his question, coffee still in hand. "Well. I guess there are several reasons. I love the look; I find comfort in the shade, and I like the symbolism of the tree."

"What's that? The symbolism, I mean."

She set her cup down and answered him. "The Japanese associate these trees with the transitory aspect of life. Happenings are short-lived in the grand scheme of things. For me, I'm grateful for the short-ness of the hard conditions I've been through. I think it's taken me a while, but the pain of it all has given me an appreciation for how amazing life is now. I love the view Jesus has given me on life now. I feel like a cherry tree has bloomed overnight inside of me—if that makes any sense."

"I think it does—sort of like there is new life inside of you now."

"Yes!" The smile on her face was brilliant. It lit her whole face up with a glow Tate wasn't sure he'd ever seen before. Tana nodded toward his cup. "I guess I'll be marrying a coffee lightweight, huh?"

Tate looked at his cup and laughed. "Just a half-step from hot chocolate. I guess I was in the mood for something sweet this morn-ing." Tana giggled with him. "I have something I would like to give a shot this morning."

Tana raised an eyebrow. "Oh?"

"How do you feel about New York?"

"New York? For our honeymoon?"

"Brooklyn, specifically. You know, my uncle once said your specialty is kids in trouble. Specifically, trafficked kids."

"He's not wrong."

"Good. I have another case I would like some help with. After the honeymoon."

Author's Note

I would like to share with you the *why* behind the story you just read and how writing *Montana Grace* moved my heart.

The idea for *Montana Grace* was born from a few things God dared to drop in my lap over ten years. I had a nice, comfortable Christian life. My friends were all Christians, and together, we looked for ways to serve our communities—through women's ministry, music ministry, church staff, and more. But God wanted me to go deeper, to be stretched, to learn to connect to Him in more tangible ways.

The first one was a dream, or nightmare, involving the kidnapping of my little girl (who was three at the time). I woke up with all the feelings—panic, sadness, and fear—running circles in my mind. My first reaction was to pray, "God, protect her from such an ordeal! Please, don't ever let anything like that happen to her." In the middle of that prayer, I heard, "What if I want to use her to bring him to me?"

"Wait, what? Yeah, I'm out of this conversation, God!" So, I set my thoughts aside and went about my day as a mom of then four kids ages eight and under. However, those thoughts, that idea, never really went away.

Next, God began to plant pictures in my mind over several years. They would play out over and over and over until I had to write them out. But then they would sit, sometimes for as long as six to seven years. Ugh. Even though the story sat, there was much research I sifted through during that time.

Lastly, some kids from our church went on several different mission trips. When they returned, they talked about all they had done. One of them said, "God doesn't just want to save the prostitutes, but also the pimps and johns." As soon as I heard the words, I remembered my dream, and I knew where the story was going.

"Okay, okay. I hear you!" I said to God. And *Montana Grace* was born.

Stats and figures are overwhelming. I'm not a numbers person, so when someone starts talking about large numbers, my eyes glaze over, and my brain goes to the beach. I cannot wrap my head around stats and figures. But let me see the pain in a little child's eyes, and my momma's heart rips open. Let me hear the horror some people live through, and I cannot sit still.

You have read the fictional story, but let's look deeper into the truth of our world today. Stats show trafficking covers several areas, like sexual exploitation, forced labor, forced begging, forced marriage, and more. In addition, children are sold as child sex slaves and child soldiers, while trafficked adults are bodies for organ harvesting. Sex trafficking is human trafficking for sexual exploitation. It includes sexual slavery, also considered modern slavery today.

For those who are numbers people, let me give a glimpse of reality:

- There are an average of 40.3 million people being trafficked worldwide.

- 24.9 million: the number of people trafficked for forced labor in the private economy. (Private economy includes: private individuals, groups, or companies in all sectors except the commercial sex industry).
- 4.8 million: the number of people trafficked for forced sexual exploitation.
- The average lifespan of a trafficking victim is seven to ten years from when they started.
- Women and girls are disproportionately affected by human trafficking, accounting for 71 percent of all victims. In addition, 25 percent of victims are children in forced labor, sex trafficking, and even forced marriage.
- The average age of domestic sex trafficking victims is fourteen years old.

Sex trafficking is extremely lucrative compared with other forms of slavery. For example, stats show sex trafficking creates half of the total profits generated globally by modern slavery, despite only accounting for 5 percent of all trafficking victims worldwide. The immense profitability of sex trafficking comes from the minimal expense of acquiring victims versus victims sold twenty times a day, generating thousands of dollars in profit per victim. Yes, you read that correctly, women and girls sold for sex twenty, thirty, and even forty times a day. Each one, each day.

I wanted to put a face, so to speak, to the problem—eyes to see the pain through. But unfortunately, there are so many real stories we do not hear while living in the safety of our suburban homes. And if we don't know the problem, our hearts will never move us to action.

The following stories are from people working to solve the problem before us. Boots on the ground, so to speak. I am grateful they took the time to share their experiences so we can help build them up together. Together, we can make a difference. Together, we can change lives.

- Stats from safehorizon.org
- Stats from togetherfreedom.org/trafficking-facts-statistics/

Why I Work with Operation Underground Railroad

by Dan Preece

For years, leading up to 2020, I had watched my old childhood friend, Jack Saunders, mention repeatedly on Facebook his connection to and support for Operation Underground Railroad. Over time, I started listening more to his message about the horrors of child sex trafficking and the amazing work being carried out by O.U.R., supported by many different fundraisers and events. Coincidentally, my professional life as a foot and ankle surgeon had finally settled down around then, and I had the beginnings of an itch to do more charity work as well as the desire to further explore my artistic side. When the pandemic hit and the shutdowns that came with it happened, I finally had the time to start exploring my options.

One day, I began watching Operation Underground Railroad YouTube videos, often presentations by Tim Ballard, the founder of O.U.R.. He mentioned the story of the young boy in Haiti who was lost to sex traffickers and whose father was constantly in search of him.

My heart was torn as I listened to the painful stories of loss but also the triumphs of many children rescued as a result of the search for that boy. As a father myself—currently of four children under fifteen years old—the stories were especially personal and motivating. I began to search for ways that I could help the cause with my limited time.

In the fall of 2019, my nephew Hyrum was living with me and out of the blue, he asked if I wanted to go in with him on a wood lathe. We started making projects and after a while, I made a bowl I was proud of and sold for $20 on Etsy. I donated the proceeds to O.U.R.. I started doing some acrylic painting along with the wood-working—and later, resin projects—and sold these projects from time to time, eventually developing a YouTube channel.

In the spring of 2021, Nikki Jelito, a fellow O.U.R. supporter suggested we start an "Etsy for O.U.R. Fundraising." We soon started ArtForOUR.org and joined ranks with Jennifer Blimka, who was making and selling jewelry for O.U.R., and Susie Webster, a very motivated volunteer. We have grown since then and recently hit our one-year anniversary. We now have over eighty contributing artists, a YouTube channel that has reached millions of viewers, and have raised almost $50,000 for Operation Underground Railroad.

Over the last year or so, we have collaborated with multiple other groups raising money for O.U.R. who were in need of items to auction and sell.

We hope to grow more and help O.U.R. rescue more children each year through our fundraising. We are always looking for more artists, more donors, and more volunteers at ArtForOUR.org! The need is great and we are motivated to continue on!

If you would like to learn more about O.U.R. or Dan, you can contact him at artforour@gmail.com *or 801-532-1822.*

Why I Fight at 81

by Mitzi Perdue (Mrs. Frank Perdue), author, speaker, businesswoman

People sometimes ask me why, at age eighty-one (and proud of it), I'm still spending ten-hour days doing what I can to combat human trafficking.

Here's the answer: Like many of us, I would like at the end of my days to feel that I tried to do something to make the world a better place.

Once I had that goal, I had to figure out how to do it best. The first question is, where is the greatest need? And the second is, where is there a match between what I can contribute and what the need is?

My first choice would be to bring about world peace; but alas, that job isn't on offer. I can't think of any way I could make a difference in that realm. So what was my second choice?

The Greatest Need

When I look around the world and see the suffering of modern slavery, it tears at my heart. According to the United Nations, there are forty million people who are enslaved today. Some are labor-trafficked; some are sex-trafficked, and some are both.

Slavery seems to me to be evil in its purest form. The suffering is unimaginable. Think of a twelve-year-old girl who's sex-trafficked and forced to have sex with strangers a dozen times a night to meet her quota. Odds are she'll be dead within seven years, a victim of an overdose, disease, suicide, or organ harvesting.

Or think of the person forced to work in a mine with no safety provisions and whose life expectancy is only a few years.

The Evil Equation

As I studied why this is happening, it became clear to me that there's an "Evil Equation" at work. There are spectacular profits to be made from slavery, and there's almost no deterrence.

Spectacular Illegal Profits + No Deterrence = Unimaginable Suffering and Death

For example, in Manhattan today, a sex trafficker with four girls can make a million dollars a year, tax-free. His chances of doing jail time are small. He knows how to keep the girls from testifying against him through threats against them or their families. Global estimates are that the chance of a trafficker doing jail time is less than one in one hundred.

What can be done to end this grisly, inhumane suffering?

In talking with at least a hundred anti-trafficking organizations, I've learned that most would like more funding and more awareness. To help raise awareness, I've written more than a hundred articles in publications, such as *Psychology Today* or the *Association of Foreign Press Correspondents*. The articles focus on the different agencies, and they use my articles for fundraising. I've been on almost two hundred podcasts. I've also helped raise more than $250,000, and I'm just getting started!

However, as of now, I want to change my focus from doing whatever I can to help individual organizations to something more holistic. What if we could eliminate human trafficking in one country, using all the knowledge and experience from academics and practitioners from around the world?

It would take years, but in the end, we'd have more knowledge than ever before of what works and what doesn't. This knowledge of best practices could be used throughout the world so instead of playing whack-a-mole, we could eliminate it everywhere.

The UBS Optimus Foundation is spearheading this effort. Their holistic approach would include rescue, restoration, prevention, deterrence, and every known method for combatting trafficking.

The country they've chosen for this pioneering effort is Bangladesh. Several countries would have liked to have been the focus of this effort, but Bangladesh won because they had governmental cooperation at the highest level, robust and effective local anti-trafficking organizations, and a civil society committed to addressing root causes.

The problems Bangladesh faces are acute. With a population of 163 million, it's one of the most densely-populated countries in the world. Poverty has encouraged such evils as bonded labor or parents who can't afford to feed their children, and the only choice available to them may be selling their children to traffickers.

Another underlying driver is an almost total lack of deterrence. "Of 6000 people arrested in the last few years," points out Nalini Tarakeshwar from Optimus, "only 25 did time. That translates into a prosecution rate of less than four per 1000. It's appalling."

Optimus is bringing together experts, practitioners, and funders. What I hope to contribute to this is that I've written a soon-to-be published biography of the *Chicken Soup for the Soul* guy, Mark Victor Hansen. He's in the *Guinness Book of World Records*, along with his co-author Jack Canfield, for having sold half a billion books.

Mark told me he expects the biography I'm writing to sell at least a million books. He's hoping for three million. It's not lost on me that this could mean a lot of money.

I'm pledging the royalties I make from the book to anti-trafficking efforts. The lion's share of the royalties will go to the Optimus efforts to end human trafficking in one country, as a way of learning how to end it in every country. If this interests you, please contact me at Mitzi@MitziPerdue.com.

Why I Did What I Did

by Derri Smith, founder and CEO Emeritus of AncoraTN

God uses brokenness to heal brokenness. It was God's will and pleasure that my brokenness become a consuming motivation to lead others to healing.

I grew up in the gang-infested neighborhoods of New York City and Philadelphia, where I was the only white girl in Black and Puerto Rican communities. My "normal" environment was shaped by the violence and intimidation of gang rivalries. These places reeled from the proclamations and then assassinations of Malcolm X and Martin Luther King Jr.. In this incubator of chaos, insecurity, and conflicting ideologies, I saw how unempowered young people became pawns for manipulation and exploitation.

As for me, personally, I was sexually abused by my father from age eleven until I left home at sixteen. My father was a pastor, the trusted man in the community. My response was to be a full-fledged hippie, dabbling in drugs and looking for love in all the wrong places. One kind man named Dub Orr took an interest in me and my dysfunctional family. He arranged a scholarship for me at Abilene Christian

College (now University.) There I met my husband, and the trajectory of my life changed. Without the interest of that one man, I could well have become a human trafficking victim. I was ripe for exploitation.

After my own long healing process, I was invited to speak about sex abuse in the church, long before it became the public topic it is today. Women came out of the woodwork telling me, often for the first time, about their own abuse, and I listened and cried with them and learned.

In the mid-'80s, I led an inner-city ministry in Nashville's low-income Edgehill neighborhood. Befriending families in the subsidized housing project, I launched a girls' club. I yearned for solutions to the cycle of kids who were born to fourteen-year-old mothers, generation after generation, and the vulnerability that comes with it. I wanted to encourage these girls that they have a higher calling than being tossed about by circumstance and by those who take advantage.

In 1986, a man named Ross—someone I knew only by reputation—stepped off a flight from his home in New Zealand and came directly to the home of our friends, Bob and Peggy Hughey. There, a group gathered for a regular Bible study. Soon after Ross entered the house, he looked across the room directly at me and waded through people seated on the floor to get to me. He bent down and spoke in a natural voice, not intending to draw attention or sound impressive.

He said, "God will use you to lead many women to freedom." Those words burned into me like a hot iron. I didn't know what it meant. Was my current work with Edgehill girls where this would happen?

In the late '80s and early '90s, Bill and I lived six years overseas helping the refugees who streamed out of Communist Eastern Europe. Maybe this is where that word would be fulfilled. A few years after the Berlin Wall fell, we returned to Nashville, now with two children of our own. To be honest, I came home not feeling like I had led many women to freedom since most of my time overseas was spent caring for our own daughters.

In 2007, with our younger daughter nearly done with high school, I asked God, "What's next?" Then, one day, I read a book about child abuse in the church, and one of the chapters was on human trafficking. That chapter left me sobbing. This was exploitation beyond my worst imaginings. From that point, I was determined to learn everything I could.

I have what my Jewish relatives call *chutzpah*, so I started calling everyone around the country working to end human trafficking and heal survivors. (That call list was very short.) I visited agencies in other parts of the country as well as those in related work with prostituted women or traumatized youth.

One Sunday, I asked at my church if anyone would like to meet that week to talk about what we could do. To my complete surprise, eighty-five people showed up. This was the first of an army of volunteers, crossing church denominations, later joined by professional staff, who sought how to be the difference in Middle Tennessee. Though still not a formal local organization, our mission was to promote healing of human trafficking survivors and strategically confront slavery in our state.

At first, we were all volunteers. We worked out of my house and out of car trunks, and we often "rented space" at Starbucks. We had no money, no connections, no clout. But we had a lot of work to do, because legislators and law enforcement told me that human trafficking didn't happen in their districts.

One day, I received a phone call from the president of the faith-based agency that Bill and I worked with in Europe. He brought me on as the first director of End Slavery Ministries, charged with training, equipping, and strategizing with global teams to address the human trafficking they encountered. I was also allowed the freedom to foster End Slavery Tennessee as an outlet for my passion to serve my own community. But my heart was already full for the girls here in the Nashville area who were lured by traffickers and sold for sex. So, I eventually retreated from the international work and charged headlong into local efforts, forming a non-profit with the help of wise people. We hired a case worker and were officially serving local survivors of human trafficking.

By the time I retired in 2020 due to my health, we had helped over a thousand survivors find the path to healing. I finally understood those words uttered in the '80s by a jet-lagged stranger from New Zealand. With the help of many volunteers and staff, God actually did use my brokenness to lead many women to freedom.

Community at Its Best

by Stacia Freeman, EPIC Girl

I believe we have a unique opportunity to pour into each other. An honest, authentic relationship is a catalyst for lasting change, and when it's reciprocated in healthy ways, that connection is life-changing. None of us are the sum of our worst choices, and God says we are all worthy of redemption.

I have served in non-profit leadership since 2006, being drawn to non-profit when I learned of the human trafficking issue and feeling a tremendous calling to do something. As a result, I led the global anti-trafficking agency from a $40,000 initiative to an over $2 million initiative through the orchestration of a merger with other agencies committed to similar work.

While I felt compassion for those victims served, my heart was always toward prevention, and I felt a tug to get directly involved in program work. I believe that if kids have the correct information to stay safe and healthy, they will.

In 2015, I implemented a curriculum in collaboration with the juvenile court to educate every female, age twelve to seventeen, on safety, and trauma and connect them to community resources. That pilot program led me to start EPIC Girl.

EPIC Girl exists to help girls find their voices. I want to be part of that and know that this journey home is about linking arms and guiding each other. Life is sweeter when it's lived out in community. EPIC Girl has taught me to live "loving my neighbor as myself," no matter how uncomfortable or challenging. And in that space with girls searching for meaning, I've found my purpose.

Heart work is the most challenging work but worthy work. In the midst of inviting someone to take a risk on love and relationship when they've had bad experiences before, I've found it's actually you that's changing. That pouring out of self, pouring ourselves out like a liquid offering before Him, changes us completely, making us more like Him.

At EPIC Girl, we believe relationships are the catalyst that drives real change. Since 2015, EPIC Girl has served over twelve hundred girls through education, safety screens, and case management.

Many of the girls we see are not ready for change, but we can plant seeds that remind them they are worthy of hope and a future. Then we trust God to do the work of making it grow. Again, I fully believe we were created to connect, and life is best lived in the company of others. EPIC Girl is that family for many of the girls we meet.

EPIC Girl works alongside other world changers, often drawing from their own experiences, to lead and nurture girls toward becoming the heroines they were created to be.

You can learn more at www.epicgirl.net.

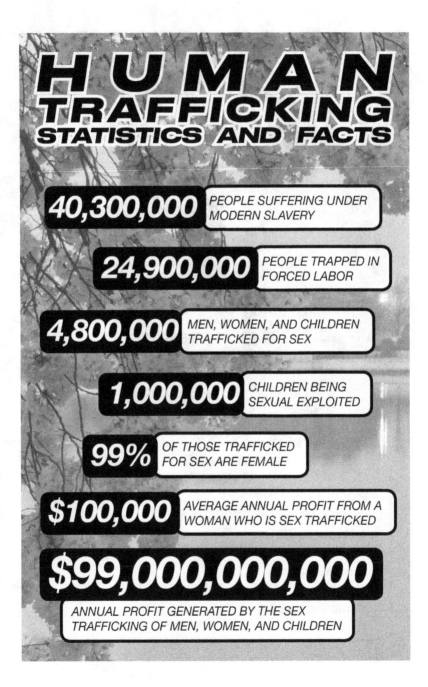

10-30 NUMBER OF TIMES TRAFFICKED WOMEN ARE FORCED TO HAVE SEX PER DAY

14 AVERAGE AGE OF TEENAGE GIRLS THAT ENTER SEX TRAFFICKING

7-10 ESTIMATED NUMBER OF YEARS A PERSON SURVIVES AFTER BEING TRAFFICKED FOR THE FIRST TIME

SOURCES

INTERNATIONAL LABOR ORGANIZATION
https://www.ilo.org/global/topics/forced-labour/lang--en/index.htm

ENOUGH.ORG
https://www.enough.org/stats-sex-trafficking

2DATE4LOVE.COM
https://2date4love.com/sex-trafficking-statistics/

HUMAN RIGHTS FIRST
https://www.humanrightsfirst.org/resource/human-trafficking-numbers

TOGETHER FREEDOM
https://togetherfreedom.org/trafficking-facts-statistics/

About The Author

Elizabeth Bradshaw grew up in Wyoming and attended a small college in Kansas to play soccer and study journalism. It was here she met Jesus. Bradshaw finished schooling in Missouri to obtain a degree in Journalism. She felt led to Nashville, Tennessee in 1993 as a twenty-two-year-old single woman fresh out of college. Currently, she lives in Franklin, Tennessee, with her husband of twenty-four years and their six fantastic children.

A free ebook edition is available with the purchase of this book.

To claim your free ebook edition:

1. Visit MorganJamesBOGO.com
2. Sign your name CLEARLY in the space
3. Complete the form and submit a photo of the entire copyright page
4. You or your friend can download the ebook to your preferred device

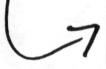

Morgan James
BOGO™

A **FREE** ebook edition is available for you or a friend with the purchase of this print book.

CLEARLY SIGN YOUR NAME ABOVE

Instructions to claim your free ebook edition:
1. Visit MorganJamesBOGO.com
2. Sign your name CLEARLY in the space above
3. Complete the form and submit a photo of this entire page
4. You or your friend can download the ebook to your preferred device

Print & Digital Together Forever.

Snap a photo

Free ebook

Read anywhere